HELLFIRE CLUB - SUTCLIFFE
AN IMMORTAL WARRIORS NOVEL
Copyright © 2022 by Sara MacKenzie
eBook 978-0-6456101-0-9
Paperback 978-0-6456101-1-6

This is a work of fiction. Names, characters, places and in-cidents are either the product of the author's imagination or are used fictitiously, and any resemblance to actual per-sons, living or dead, business establishments, events or lo-cales is entirely coincidental.

Printed in the USA.

Cover Design and Interior Format

HELLFIRE CLUB: SUTCLIFFE

AN IMMORTAL WARRIORS NOVEL

SARA MACKENZIE

At last I give you Sutcliffe!
I hope the wait was worth it.

Prologue

1808 Blackfriars Abbey,
Lincolnshire, England

AIDEN SUTCLIFFE WAS awake and alert, but he wasn't sure how long he would remain so. Both of his friends, Charles Escott, the Marquis of Lorne and Nicholas Darlington, Earl of Northcote, had been sent to their death-like sleep by the Sorceress. Now only he remained. He and his faithful dog, Loki.

Their stupidity had brought this about, and a tiny voice in Aiden's head warned him that he had known all along they had been paddling in some very dangerous waters. And yet he had said nothing.

"Aiden Lord Sutcliffe," the witch said in a sing-song voice.

He winced.

"Aiden is so agreeable. A friend to all. Will we ride our horses at top speed through the village, risking life and limb? Aiden says yes. Will we drink countless bottles of wine and play silly games in the crypt? Aiden says yes. Will we invite a demon from the dark realms into the mortal world? Aiden says, why not?"

He glanced up and forced himself to meet her eyes. What he saw in their depths was so much worse than he'd anticipated.

"You allow yourself to drift along in life, Lord Sutcliffe. You never make waves. You never engage deeply in anything. You skim the surface of your existence. One could almost call you apathetic. Why is that? Do you believe you have no right to your own opinions? Or do you not trust yourself to have an opinion?"

"I don't see the point in arguing," he said without emotion.

Loki whined and circled at Aiden's feet. The wolflike dog wanted to leave and Aiden didn't blame him, but there was no going anywhere now. It was too late for that. Lorne and Darlington had been delivered into their long sleep, and soon he would follow.

"No point in arguing?" the witch's voice had grown softer yet more menacing. "Even when you could have saved yourself and your friends from these dire consequences? You knew that what Lorne was doing was wrong. Darlington was probably too drunk to notice but you knew, Lord Sutcliffe, yet you did nothing."

"It wouldn't have mattered if I had disagreed. Why should I fall out with my friend when the outcome was never in doubt? Lorne does what Lorne does."

She cocked her head to one side. "I think you underestimate yourself, Aiden. I think if you had wanted to make your arguments—and you are good at that, I know you are—then Lorne would have listened to you. You may be right when you say he would not have acted any differently, but how will we ever know? You should have tried."

Aiden said nothing.

"Couldn't you be bothered?" she asked mockingly.

"It is safer not to rock the boat. Good intentions can end in bad outcomes. That is just the way it is. If I had tried to force him to my point of view and it had gone wrong…"

He'd said too much, and he stopped himself before he said more. Too late, of course, because he saw the flare in her eyes as she latched on to his mistake.

"And then if it had gone wrong…?" Her voice dropped even more. "Then what?"

Loki whined and nudged against his thigh, but Aiden couldn't take his eyes from the witch. Was something moving there in those azure depths? He shuddered, and the words were pulled from his lips.

"It would have been my fault."

She seemed pleased.

"So rather than making an effort to avert a disastrous outcome, you chose to step back and allow it to happen. I wouldn't have considered you a coward, Aiden. You are certainly not a physical coward. You fought just as hard as the other two to bring the Destroyer to me. What is it then? What are you protecting?"

He couldn't answer her. There was a lock inside

him, and he had not turned that key since he was five years of age. Even this terrifying woman would not make him do it.

"So be it," she said. "But be warned, Aiden, there will come a time when you will need to make a choice between holding your secrets and setting them free."

"You know nothing of me."

She smiled at the stubborn note in his voice. "I wouldn't say nothing. But it is true, you have strong walls. I think I will enjoy breaking them." She stepped closer, and the power that surrounded her made his head spin sickeningly. "And have no doubt, my lord, I will break them down."

"You can try," he said, and wondered why he was goading her. Suddenly he realised how sick of himself he was, how tired of everything. Was she right? Was he a coward? Could he have stopped Lorne's insanity?

A smile twitched the Sorceress's lips and Loki whined again.

"Please," he said. "Will you spare my dog?"

She chuckled. "So you will not beg for your own life, but you will for your pet? I find that strangely hopeful."

"So you will let Loki go?"

She seemed to consider before she shook her head. "No. You need each other, more than you know. You will sleep together until you need to fight again. Prepare yourself, Aiden."

His head swam, and the darkness lurched toward him. He felt his life narrow, spinning backwards.

He was five years old again. Helpless, alone, and about to be broken.

Chapter One

Present Day, Isle of Moyle,
Scotland

"GO AWAY, YOU wretched mutt!"
    Alison MacDonald-Ellis blocked the
doorway in an attempt to keep the animal out,
but Loki wasn't having any of that. He leapt up,
making her take a step back, and before she knew
it, the dog was inside her cottage.

"Again?" she said grumpily. The couple who
had been here earlier—Nicholas and Linny—had
claimed the animal as theirs and taken it away
with them. Or so she'd hoped. Strangers on the
island, the two had said they were lost. They were
attending the ceilidh on Saturday night and she
had set them on the right path back to the town
and the hotel.

She paused a moment, wondering if they had
found themselves in any difficulty. It had been
strange seeing them here in such weather, and
they had been hardly dressed for it. She'd half
wondered if they were ghosts from another time,
especially the man. He'd even had the old-fash-

ioned manners of a gentleman from long ago.

Loki danced around her, whining, knocking things over. She caught him by the collar and saw that it was the same impromptu one she had given them, a knitted rope. It had broken off, and the dog was trailing a foot of it behind.

She huffed. "So you ran away, you wretched animal." She dragged him toward the laundry. "Well, you can stay in here. I won't have you destroying anything else, thank you very much."

The dog wriggled and tried to escape, giving a desperate stare over her shoulder. So desperate that Ally was convinced he'd seen something. She turned to look, only to feel like a fool. The room was empty. Nothing to see because of course it was, she lived alone. With an impatient sigh, she hauled the dog into the laundry and closed the door. Almost immediately, it began to scrabble on the wood with its claws.

Wonderful.

She still had several garments to complete before Saturday night. Luckily, the manager of the hotel had agreed to let her set up a pop-up shop in their foyer, and her team of knitters were working overtime to get everything ready. She'd been assured that the guests were well-heeled, so it would be worth the extra hours. They might make some sales, but that wasn't as important as the chance to create a buzz for her business. Word of mouth could make them a success overnight.

In the laundry room, Loki began to howl.

Ally put her hands over her ears and groaned. "Stop it!"

She turned, intending to return to her seat by the fire, just as something brushed by her.

Something big. Far bigger than a dog.

Ally froze.

But the room was empty. She could see with her own eyes that she was alone, yet at the same time she knew with every fibre of her being that someone else was in here with her. Someone or something. Was that what was wrong with the dog? Did it sense whoever was in here?

"Who are you?" she demanded, as if she weren't frightened out of her wits. Ally had had the sight since she was a child, but she had never been comfortable with it and had certainly never wanted it. It was just something that was part of her, like the auburn of her hair or her green eyes. The truth was, she'd hoped she had left this awkward sixth sense behind her. Until now, her isolated cottage had been safe from the "other."

"Answer me." She folded her arms as if she were in charge, a trick she'd learned as a child to hide her fear. It usually worked. The "other" were confused by mortals who did not scream and run.

Something shifted in the atmosphere, as if the air had been displaced by a large presence. Then a voice spoke, though the sound was inside her head rather than in the room. Not unusual. She had been hearing voices most of her life. But what was unusual was that it was a very deep, aristo-cratic male voice. It sent shivers up her spine that were more astonishment than fear.

"I am Sutcliffe. Please, help me."

Despite her certainty that she was not alone, Ally

hadn't really expected a response. For a moment, she felt quite dizzy. Why was this happening to her? She'd been running from her abilities for years, and Moyle was one of the farthest outposts in the United Kingdom. It had seemed like a good place to hide. She had been here for over a year, living peacefully, and this was the first time one of the "other" had tracked her down.

She took a steadying breath. "Sutcliffe? Sut–cliffe who?"

"Aiden Sutcliffe." He made a deep grumbling noise, as if this situation were as annoying for him as it was for her.

A newly released soul, perhaps? They were often confused, especially if their death had been sudden and they didn't yet know that they were dead. Perhaps if she took him back to the moment of his passing, he would accept his new state and she could send him on his way.

"Where were you before this?"

Another grumble.

"Try to remember, Aiden."

"I was in Port Finlay with my friends. We drove up from Glasgow because there was a situation."

The name sounded familiar. "You mean the town where everybody has vanished? I heard they were all back again." Moyle might be a long way from the rest of Scotland, but like everyone in the Outer Hebrides, Ally had broadband, and could keep up with current affairs. The story had been intriguing, and despite all the experts having their say, no one yet had explained the phenomenon to her satisfaction.

"Were they?" There was a pause while he took that in, then another sigh. "When we got to Port Finlay, we were stopped by the army… the police. Both. There was an explosion."

Ally remembered seeing the aftermath on the newsfeed on her laptop, but the reporter insisted no one was hurt. There had been no reports of anyone dying. Had the authorities kept that from the public?

"And after the explosion?" she asked gently.

"After the explosion, I woke up here. With you. My friends were gone, but Loki was with me. Loki is my dog. The one you have locked up."

She had been beginning to formulate a story for the poor man. Clearly, he had died in the explosion and somehow his spirit had zeroed in on her—it had happened before. The dead tended to seek out those who could help them once they'd realised it was pointless hanging around the scene of their death.

But then he'd mentioned the wretched dog and thrown that theory out of the window.

"Loki?" she repeated in a startled voice. "But… he's not dead."

"No, he's very much alive. I should warn you that he's never been keen on being confined in small spaces. He will tear that door to pieces."

There was a hint of humour in his voice and she felt herself respond. Ridiculous, because this man was a ghost. An invisible ghost.

"How can your dog be here?" She pushed aside her inconvenient thoughts. "Wasn't he caught in the explosion with you? Port Finlay is on the mainland and Moyle is an island. You'd have to take more than one ferry to get here, or fly from Glasgow."

"All that I know is we were all in Port Finlay. Two of my friends, the ones who were here earlier, took Loki with them. I tried to make them see or hear me, but to no avail." The frustration in his deep voice was unmistakable.

"Your friends?" She was starting to sound like a parrot, yet she couldn't seem to help it.

"Nicholas and Linny. They were with me in Port Finlay when the explosion happened. Now they're here. Look,"—she could imagine him running his hands through his hair in frustration—"just make me visible again and I can find my friends."

That made her laugh. "I would if I could, believe me! I should explain something to you, Aiden. I am one of those people who can communicate with the dead. And since I can't see you, that must be what you are. Dead."

There was a silence and she felt guilty. "Sorry. I should have broken it to you in a gentler fashion."

"But it isn't true," he said quietly. "I'm not dead. That is, I am dead, but I was already dead before I came back to life." He sighed, recognising how his words sounded like nonsense to her. "My friends… If you can get me to them, they will be able to help me. Or the Sorceress," he added hopefully.

"The Sorceress?" she repeated carefully. Brilliant. She was lumbered with a ghost with serious mental issues.

Another grumble. "I can tell you don't believe me. Would you let me in to see Loki at least? I can calm him down. He's worried about me."

It seemed a reasonable request, and the dog was tearing her laundry door apart. Although it did occur to her that if he was really a ghost, he should be able to walk through it. That was the issue of the newly dead, though. They were unaware of their abilities.

As she opened the door, Loki made a terrible moan and launched himself into the air. Ally cried out, thinking the dog would fall to the ground in a heap. But to her surprise, he was caught and held by… nothing.

She could see Loki's tongue lap at whatever held him and hear the murmured endearments from his invisible master.

She stood and watched in utter astonishment. No ghost she had ever seen had been capable of this. It appeared that Aiden Sutcliffe, her invisible friend, was a something she had never dealt with before.

Chapter Two

AIDEN HEAVED A sigh of relief as he closed his arms around his faithful companion. Loki was alive, and even if Aiden was still unsure about what exactly was happening to him, he was alive too. If only he could rejoin the others, or at least make himself visible.

Since he had arrived yesterday, he'd been watching the red-haired woman. He'd tried to make contact with her. At first he had thought she was ignoring him, but he soon discovered she genuinely couldn't see or hear him, until now. But there had been a few occasions when she seemed to sense something and glanced up, staring at the spot where he had been seated. Or when she had stepped into his space, she would look about wildly. Having her more or less inside his body had made him feel very queasy.

His growing frustration had made him want to scream, and he had wondered whether this was to be his future, some new torture the Sorceress had devised for him. Then Nicholas Darlington and Linny McNab had arrived.

He'd thought he was saved. In his excitement,

he'd shouted out their names, rushing toward them, only to find that they couldn't see or hear him either. In desperation, he'd tried to grab hold of Nicholas and shake him, but his hand had gone right through his friend's shoulder.

It had been a sobering moment.

He'd wondered if he truly was a ghost, no longer existing in the mortal world. After they had left the cottage, he had tried to follow them, only to be thwarted once again by his new condition. Two steps beyond the gate and he had run into a cold, damp, foggy wall. He'd pushed at it, moved along it, searching for a way through, but it went all the way around the cottage.

The experience had been most unpleasant and, if he was honest, rather frightening.

The following hours had been some of the worst he had ever experienced. He began to believe he was trapped in this godforsaken place forever more. All he could see outside the windows were grey clouds and sleety winds throwing rain against the glass. From the conversations he overheard the red-haired woman have on her phone, he knew he was on the Island of Moyle. Simon Frazer's island home. He'd seen some business cards lying on a side table with her name—Alison (Ally) MacDonald-Ellis—with her address on them, and that had confirmed it.

However, Aiden Sutcliffe couldn't stay glum for long. He was naturally, on the surface at least, a sunny sort of personality. He tried to bolster his spirits, reminding himself that at least Nicholas and Linny were still alive. After the explosion at

Port Finlay, he'd been in the dark about what had happened to his friends. He still didn't know the fate of Lorne and Maggie, however.

Trapped in this place, with no way of escape or of being seen and heard, Aiden had had plenty of time to think about what had happened in Port Finlay.

The explosion had been Stewart's doing, Aiden was sure of it, but he wondered why the Sorceress wasn't helping them. Was this yet another test? Honestly, he just wanted this all to end. He longed to walk the streets of this modern world without fearing that Stewart or one of his vile accomplices might suddenly turn up and throw his calm world into chaos. He wanted this quest to be finished.

Lorne should not be made to return to the past to take the blame for their stupidity, and Aiden knew that if that did happen then he would go with the Marquis and share his fate. They were all to blame, not just Lorne, and so they should all be punished. The Sorceress was right when she'd told him he could have stopped his friend. During his long years of sleep, he had come to understand he was just as culpable.

But before he could move forward, he had to escape from this bloody cottage and rejoin his friends. And to do that, he was going to need Miss Ally MacDonald-Ellis's help. That she could now hear him and he could hold his loyal dog once again, seemed to suggest that things were improving for him. It gave him his first spark of hope.

Aiden cleared his throat. "You said you see people who have died?"

"Yes, I do."

She glanced in his direction, chewing her bottom lip. Something about her white teeth sinking into that plump pinkness reminded him how attractive she was, with her warm smile and green eyes with their thick dark lashes, not to mention her lush curves.

He pushed the distraction aside. No time for that now.

"Aiden?"

Blast, he hadn't answered her. He cleared his throat. "Are you a witch?"

Humour lit up her eyes. A lock of auburn hair fell across her smooth cheek and she tucked it back. "No, I'm not. I think of myself as a genetic freak, although at school I was just called the 'freak' part." She sobered and leaned forward. "I can see the dead and communicate with them. It's not something I learned in a book of spells."

"Hmm." He'd seen a movie about that, hadn't he? But movies, as Maggie had explained to him, were like novels in pictures. They were not real. Ally seemed to genuinely believe what she said.

She was expanding on her statement now, her voice eager. "When someone dies, they can become confused, especially if they die suddenly. When they come to me, I try to help them find their way to wherever it is they are meant to be." She hesitated. "Are you sure you're not…?"

"I am sure," he said firmly. "I am not dead." Then he spoilt it by adding, "Well, not entirely. I was asleep for two hundred years."

"Two hundred years?" she repeated. "But that makes you…?"

"Old, yes." He gave a chuckle. "My companions and I lay in dormant slumber, waiting to be woken by the Sorceress when she had need of us…"

Ally had forgotten to blink.

"It's complicated," Aiden added lamely. He ran a hand through his hair and wished he had a gift with words the way Lorne did. Would Ally believe him? He needed her trust if he was to get back to his friends.

She was looking at him with such intensity that it was difficult to remember she couldn't actually see him.

"Let me try something," she said after a moment. She took a step forward and then another and reached out, just as he stepped toward her. She collided with him, her face squishing against his chest, and her breath went out with an umph.

He caught her arms, holding her steady. When she'd regained her balance, she lifted her face and stared up at him with wide green eyes surrounded by those thick dark lashes. As tall as she was, he was still taller. He had a perfect view of the scatter of freckles across her nose and cheeks, and those pink, lush lips. She was fresh faced and lovely, and a citrusy scent emanated from her auburn hair that made his mouth water.

"Sorry," he said, discomforted. "I should have realised that you could feel me now."

"You're big," she said, then gave a shake of her

head as if her comment had embarrassed her. "I should have guessed that from your voice. You have one of those deep growly ones." She looked even more embarrassed when he laughed.

After a moment, he let her go and she stepped back, still looking in his direction. "Do you think that you being able to touch me and hear me means I am returning to my proper state?"

"I suppose," she said cautiously, "but given that I have never encountered a man who has been asleep for two hundred years, claims not to be dead, and is invisible but can be touched, I can't really answer you with much authority."

He liked the way she spoke. Her accent was as posh as Lorne's, and she had a way of putting her words together that led him to believe she'd been well educated. Oxford or Cambridge, perhaps. What on earth was she doing on Moyle? He was about to ask her when she interrupted him.

"Your friends, the ones you mentioned. Are they the same as you? I mean, are they…?"

"Old? Yes, Lorne and Darlington and I come from the year 1808." He was about to explain that the McNab sisters were not from the past when she interrupted him again.

"Why are you here in the future?" She spoke in a bemused tone, as if she wondered how she could possibly be having this conversation.

He sighed. "Through our own stupidity," he said. "We did something dangerous and we are here to make right a great wrong." It was more than that, he knew, but the truth was strange enough without going into too much detail.

He didn't want Ally to run screaming from the house. "The Sorceress might send us back if we fail to complete our task, but we do not want to go back. We have ties to this time now."

Ally's head tilted to one side. "I think you need to tell me your story properly. In detail. If you want my help, I need to understand what is going on." She glanced around. "Unfortunately, I have some people coming over to help finish up these garments. You'll have to wait until they're gone."

He'd noticed the piles of knitted fabric around the cottage, and had seen her busy with them earlier.

It sounded more like an order than a request, but Aiden wasn't opposed to telling her his story. What choice did he have? And perhaps she could help him get back to the others before Stewart put them into further danger. He needed to know what had happened to Lorne and Maggie. He needed to know they were safe. Because if they were going to defeat Stewart, they had to be strong. And the three of them were at their strongest when they were together.

"Can you find out where Nicholas and Linny are? Do you have a mobile phone?" Aiden had used one in Glasgow and, if he did say so himself, had become rather good at texting.

"I do," she replied, glancing toward the window as they heard the gate open and close. "But coverage is patchy and the storm always knocks it out, sometimes for days. Communication on Moyle is hardly reliable. I'm sorry." She got to her feet, moving toward the door.

She opened it and a gust of cold air came in, along with a gaggle of women of various ages, all talking at the same time. He sighed. It looked as if he was in the hands of Ally MacDonald-Ellis, and there was not much he could do to hurry things along.

Chapter Three

NICHOLAS DARLINGTON STOOD at the window and pronounced the weather even fouler than it had been five minutes ago, which was saying something. Great gusts of wind rattled the glass, and they could hear the walls moan as the squall circled the hotel building, trying to find a way inside. As usual, Lorne had procured himself the biggest suite, and though Nicholas had teased him about it, he didn't truly mind. So long as Linny was safe in his arms, he was happy to be anywhere. Apart from the Dark World, of course.

That was a place he never wished to visit again. He'd woken in a sweat last night, reliving the spin of the cages and the demon that had crept toward Linny's sleeping body. And then he lay there, wide-eyed, unable to rest, remembering the dark void that led to hell.

Although he was safe for now, anything was possible. He couldn't let himself dwell too much on what the future might hold. It was essential to focus on the here and now. They still had to defeat Stewart. Only then could he make a new life here in this modern century with the woman he loved.

A knock on their door brought him back from his dark thoughts. He turned from the window as Lorne admitted a waiter with a trolley. They'd ordered room service, and now, smelling the grilled Scottish salmon, Nicholas realised how hungry he was. He paused as he went to sit down, expecting to see Loki nearby begging for a share. But, of course, Loki wasn't here.

As they sat down to eat, a wave of anxiety swept over him as it dawned on him how much he missed Aiden Sutcliffe and his hell hound. What had happened to the man while Nicholas and Linny had been trapped in the Dark World?

"After the explosion, Maggie and I found ourselves here in Moyle," Lorne had explained earlier. "Don't ask me how. We walked into the hotel and discovered they were expecting us."

"That was when the alarm bells started ringing," Maggie had put in. "So to speak." She was still red-eyed from her emotional reunion with her sister, and they hadn't moved from their seat on the sofa, pressed close together. Nicholas wasn't quite as demonstrative with Lorne, but he was so overjoyed to see his friend he had thrown his arms around the man in a great embrace, and to his credit, Lorne had endured it for a few moments longer than he had expected him to.

They were alive and, for the moment, they were safe. Now they just needed to find Sutcliffe to reunite the Hellfire Club.

Nicholas had finished his meal when somewhere outside in the darkening sky came a muffled drone. He went to the window and peered at the clouds as something bright and arrowlike appeared, dropping sharply toward the land.

What modern wonder was this? For a moment, he felt disorientated, caught between the past and the present.

Linny jumped to her feet and came to join him. "Is the pilot insane?

Of course, he thought, an aeroplane. What sane man would climb into one?

They watched as the silver fuselage circled the town, followed by the whine of its engine. The plane was attempting to land despite the appalling weather. Either the pilot was insane, as Linny suggested, or he was skilled enough to have earned the confidence that he would not crash into the sea.

"When was Simon's cousin supposed to arrive?" Lorne asked.

Nicholas met his icy blue gaze. Professor Simon Frazer was dead, but according to the staff of the hotel, his cousin was scheduled to arrive on Moyle soon.

Except that everyone in this room knew that Simon had no cousin.

"Do you think he's on board that hell craft?" Nicholas asked.

Just as they knew Simon did not have a cousin, they suspected the mystery guest was in fact their nemesis, Stewart, the one they had been tasked to capture by the Sorceress. To stop him before he unleashed his evil upon the world. Stewart had been considered beyond redemption and destined for the underworld, but then had managed to escape. He was still at large and determined to destroy Lorne and all those he held dear. Everything that had happened up to now had been leading to this moment. Stewart's grand finale.

"Simon doesn't have a cousin," Maggie reminded them for what felt like the fiftieth time. "It has to be Stewart."

"And he will want to make the most of his final performance," Lorne agreed. "Something never to be forgotten."

"You have the ring?" Maggie asked, also for the fiftieth time.

Lorne patted his pocket. The Sorceress had given him a ring of binding to place upon Stewart's finger. Once that was done he would be held in place and she would appear and hurry him back to the Underworld. At least, that was the plan. The tricky part was actually getting the ring onto the man's finger. So far, they hadn't been able to get near enough.

Linny took Nicholas's hand and leaned against him. He tried to stop himself from sniffing her hair because, well, that was something only a sad sort of fellow would do. Although perhaps he didn't quite manage it because he heard Lorne give a sharp laugh behind them, and then heard Maggie giggle.

Linny just leaned closer and sighed.

Nicholas wasn't sure how much longer he would be able to hold this woman he loved with all his heart. If they failed to return Stewart to the Sorceress, then all three of them would go to the Underworld in his place. Even if they did capture him, they might still be returned to the year 1808 to face the consequences of their actions. The Sorceress held all the power where their future was concerned, and saw no reason to bargain with them.

"We need to find Aiden," his beloved murmured.

"We will," he said. "And after that, we will deal with our American friend."

"Why isn't the witchy woman here helping us?" Linny asked, sounding disgruntled. "I thought she was on your side."

Nicholas met Lorne's icy stare in the window's reflection and grimaced.

"That might be stretching it a bit," he said. "We are tools to her. She likes us to do the hard work and only steps in when we get it wrong."

"I wonder if even the Sorceress knows what Stewart is up to this time," Lorne added quietly, a hint of concern in his voice. "He seems to be reading her like a book. I get the impression that she is floundering, trying to catch up. It doesn't bode well."

Nicholas suddenly didn't feel so good. The salmon wasn't sitting comfortably in his stomach. He met Lorne's gaze again and knew they were both thinking the same thing.

Were they completely on their own this time?

Maggie spoke up. "We need to search the island. Every inch of it. We need to make sure he isn't already here."

Lorne walked toward her. "And what would that achieve, my love?" he asked with a hint of impatience.

"At least then we would know, Lorne."

His tone softened. "Maggie, it's not practical. Look outside. We'd be blown away. And knowing Stewart, we'd only find him if he wanted us to."

"He'd probably pick us off one by one," Nicholas muttered.

Linny butted in. "Maggie, our names were in the reservations register downstairs, right? He wants us here, in this hotel. He's counting on it. Nicholas is right, he's going to make a grand entrance, and it wouldn't be a grand entrance if we weren't here to see it. We need to lure him into a trap, but that's not going to happen if we're traipsing around in the heather with the sheep."

For a moment it seemed touch and go whether Maggie would burst into tears or hysterical laughter. In the end, she did neither. "I'd prefer the sheep to Stewart's critters," she grumbled. "At least they're friendly."

Linny snorted a laugh. "Not in my experience."

Maggie looked at the concerned faces around her and sighed. "Sorry," she said. "Pregnant woman hormones. I thought I was being rational, but I've turned into a gibbering mess."

Lorne tugged her into his arms. For a moment they were still, just holding each other. Nicholas turned back to the window to give them some privacy. Linny resumed her position by his side.

"He'll come here," she said quietly. "He doesn't

just want to beat you; he needs you to know he's your better."

"You're right." He bent closer and didn't even pretend not to press his face into her hair this time, taking in her perfumed scent. "Let's go back to our room," he said.

She cuddled closer. "Let's."

Chapter Four

———

"ALLY, WHERE DO you want me to put—?"

Ally jumped as one of the women startled her. "Oh!"

"Are you all right?" Mrs Morison eyed her with concern, her smooth unlined face belying her age. That was something Ally had noticed about Moyle, the elderly looked younger than their years. When she first came here, she'd wondered whether it was the damp climate or if some kind of magical properties existed on Moyle. She had yet to decide.

She shrugged off the other woman's disquiet. "Yes, I'm fine." It was a lie. She wasn't fine. How could she be when she had a dead man living in her house? Although the experience wasn't new to her, and Aiden Sutcliffe insisted he wasn't technically dead—even if he was over two hundred years old. As strange as his story was, she was inclined to believe him. She had felt his body against hers. A big, warm, hard body. Unless she was losing her mind completely, her invisible guest was very real.

Ally shivered. Not from the cold, though the weather outside had turned decidedly nasty. She reminded herself that she had work to do. Five of her knitting partners had arrived to finish the work they planned to take to the hotel in time for the ceilidh. There were some gorgeous pieces, and she was certain they would sell most of them and take orders for more. Yes, she was excited, and so were her ladies. They had been building this business for almost a year, ever since Ally arrived on Moyle, and this was their first chance to really shine. Yet here she was, struggling to keep her mind on the job.

She found herself glancing about as she wondered where Aiden was. He had to be here somewhere. She could feel him, but he was being awfully quiet… unlike his hellhound, which was moaning and groaning through the laundry door.

She'd told the others she was minding the beast for a neighbour. They'd exchanged sideways glances, and she remembered too late that they knew everyone on the island and would realise the dog was a stranger to Moyle.

Rather like Ally herself.

She had been on Moyle for thirteen months and most mornings she woke up with a smile on her face. Being in this isolated place was no hardship to her. She loved what she was doing, even if she wasn't as good at knitting as the women she'd brought together to form this business. She had enthusiasm enough for all of them, and a good head for the financial side of things. She'd learnt to shrug off their gentle laughter at her mistakes and admire the work they created together.

Her life now couldn't have been more different from the one she left behind in the South of England on her father's estate. Even saying 'estate' made her feel queasy. Her father was a titled gentleman, one of the landed gentry, and very eccentric. This was not unusual for titled gentlemen, but in his case, the eccentricities went further than taking a bath with his dogs or wandering around the house in women's clothing, as had been the case with a few others she'd known.

Her father was the head of a commune. His manor house, instead of hosting other titled families or even royalty, as it had in the past, had been opened up to other like-minded bohemians. It also attracted those eager to pretend to accept her father's philosophies, so that they could take advantage of the carefree lifestyle, as well as free rent and free meals, and evenings of booze and drugs.

Ally's mother had left when her daughter was barely able to walk—not that Ally blamed her. Her father was the opposite of monogamous and her mother, who'd decided she preferred monogamy, had a fiery temper. Words were said. Things were thrown. She had intended to take Ally with her, but had been thwarted by her father and a lawyer in a smart suit… and a cheque book. Her mother had left, sadder and wiser, but certainly richer.

After that, Ally had been brought up by a menagerie of girlfriends and lady hangers on. Sometimes she went to stay with her father's sister, where life was much stricter. In some ways she'd actually had a very nice childhood. She couldn't say she had been neglected or abused, at least not until she turned sixteen. Then she had learned that she was supposed to be 'the one'.

Being 'the one' hadn't meant all that much to her at first. She'd shrugged it off, just as she did most of the weird stuff that happened in her life. By then, she'd had numerous experiences with desperate ghosts and, with the help of one of her father's girlfriends, an amateur medium, she'd learned how to cope with them.

Then one day, she almost walked in on her father and his new guru. She overheard them talking, and it became clear to her what being 'the one' really entailed. After that, matters became very dark indeed.

One of the ladies held up a shoulder warmer wrap, knitted in soft blues and mauves. "What do you think?"

There were murmurs of praise and approval.

"The outlanders will love that," Ally sighed. "They'll imagine they're Claire and there is a Jamie out there somewhere waiting for them."

The women exchanged knowing chuckles, and Ally realised that with the description of their clients as 'outlanders,' she had put herself firmly on the side of the islanders. She had no problem with that.

"Right then, I think we are almost done," she added briskly, hearing her cut glass accent. It set her apart from the islanders, and yet nowadays the inhabitants of Moyle didn't seem to care.

When she had first arrived, they had looked at her askance. Her 'wild' ideas of making money with their creative talents had produced a small storm of controversy and disapproval. But Ally was good at getting around people. It was a skill she'd had to learn at an early age.

So she had waxed lyrical about showing the world what a special place Moyle was, of finding a way to give the island's women some independence. She persuaded one person, and then another, and before too long, they were all on her side. It still surprised her that she had achieved so much in so short a time.

This is my home now. And I don't care if I'm 'the one,' I'm never going back to my father and his kooky friends. I'm safe here.

This was because being 'the one' involved some extremely bleak nonsense. The conversation she'd walked in on between her father and his guru had been about the end of the world. And from what she had overheard, it was happening sooner rather than later.

The most disappointing thing was that at first, as she'd stood listening in the doorway, she had thought that she was 'the one' to save the world. That it was she who would shine a bright light on those dark forces before they could destroy everything that was good.

But as she kept listening Ally had come to understand that she was to be the catalyst and not the cure. She would bring about the end of days, a horsewoman of the apocalypse, as it were.

The two of them had noticed her then, and she

had seen the guilt on her father's face. The fear in his eyes. He wasn't any happier about the news than her, and yet she knew from experience that he wasn't going to stand up for her.

Things had never been the same after that. She had remained on the estate until she was eighteen and left for university. She'd specialised in the arts, where she could enrol in the sort of courses she was interested in, textiles and design.

For the next few years, she rarely went home. The guru had left, and her father had another mentor who was less intimidating and certainly did not speak of Ally as being 'the one.' But the relationship between herself and her father had never recovered, so she'd stayed away.

Hearing that she would be responsible for the end of the world had been a burden ever since. Others might have dismissed it as rubbish, but Ally spoke to the dead. That made it difficult to dismiss the existence of the supernatural. She felt on edge. She had terrible dreams, and began to put distance between herself and anything connected to her father, moving further and further north.

Then one day, she read a book about Moyle by Professor Simon Frazer. She was enchanted by its rough beauty, and how isolated the island was. She would be safe there, wouldn't she?

So it was ironic that once she arrived, she had created the knitting circle in the hopes of opening Moyle up to the world. Was that the right thing to do? Worry kept her awake at night, and yet hiding in her cottage and refusing to open the door did not seem like the right thing to do either.

And now this Aiden Sutcliffe had come to her, with his talk of dangerous forces and a powerful sorceress. Was this what she had been waiting for all these years? Was this the beginning of the end of days?

Chapter Five

THE KNITTING WOMEN were gathered together, laughing and talking, and Aiden could barely make out their words. The Moyle accent was a soft, sibilating one, and their sentences often ran together. In time he thought he would get used to it, but whenever they spoke quickly he was lost.

Nicholas and Linny never strayed far from his thoughts. He knew they were on the island, but where exactly? He just hoped they had reached some kind of safety and shelter before they were blown into the sea.

He remembered the moment before the explosion had happened in Port Finley with Maggie running toward the site of the blast. His chest ached at the thought that she may be dead, but he reminded himself that Loki had been running with her, and he was alive.

It was possible that Stewart would want Maggie dead to punish Lorne. But when the man had had her in his power back at Blackfriars Abbey, he hadn't harmed her. Rather, he had sent her into the past to try and turn her against Lorne. Aiden

suspected that killing someone was far too simple for a devious creature like Stewart. He would
want to take centre stage like the showman he
was. He wanted the pain to be drawn out, and he
wanted to watch it unfold, and most importantly,
he wanted to see Lorne suffer.

Aiden needed to find them. He ran a hand over
his face and groaned.

A couple of the women stopped and looked
up. "What was that?" one asked as Loki began to
bark again.

"I'm sorry," Ally said, looking a little flustered.
"I'd put him outside, but that makes him even
worse."

"He sounds almost human."

"I have been told that," Ally agreed. "What do
you think of these colours?"

The conversation started up again and Aiden
breathed a sigh of relief.

He couldn't remember a time when he had
stood quietly as a gaggle of women pursued such
hobbies. It was so far beyond his experience.
Although, since he had been awoken by the Sorceress, the range of his experiences had certainly
become more varied.

He leaned against the wall and let his gaze linger on the proceedings. That gaze lingered longer
on Ally MacDonald-Ellis than anyone else, and
he admitted to himself that he was attracted to
her. Was it her pretty face and sparkling green
eyes? Perhaps. Or perhaps it was the sound of her
voice, her husky laugh, and the warm smile she
shared with those around her. He noted the little

glances she kept shooting in his direction, as if she sensed exactly where he was standing and felt his gaze on her.

Aiden Sutcliffe was no shrinking violet, and women seemed to enjoy his dark good looks and easy manner. No one had stayed with him for long however, and he had been happy to let them go or, on occasion, gently ease them out the door. He became uncomfortable when a woman wanted more from him than a few nights in his bed. He preferred his solitude when it came to women because it meant no one could be hurt by him.

Aiden was aware there was a reason for him thinking that way. He preferred not to dwell on it. In fact, Aiden was a man who tried not to think too deeply about anything at all.

Was that why the Sorceress was punishing him now? Her words to him when she'd sent him to sleep were burned into his brain. And there had been the dreams... He shuddered at the memory of them. The witch had taken him back into the past over and over, pushing him, urging him to confront his pain, until he had screamed for her to leave him alone. Screamed and wept like a child.

The discomforting memory made him flush with embarrassment.

Oh yes, the witch had done her best to break down his walls, yet he had managed to hold that piece of himself back. A tiny kernel clasped in his fist. He thought she hadn't noticed, but he was beginning to think he had been very foolish to underestimate her. She was intent on tearing him open, and he was filled with a sense of dread whenever he thought about what would happen once that last secret was finally exposed. Would he survive it?

There was a plucking at the back of his neck, like scratchy fingers running down his spine. His body went stiff. Something was behind him and he knew, even before he turned, who it was. That presence was unmistakable, the atmosphere charged with awe and terror.

The Sorceress stood inside the room to his left, a soft blue light surrounding her, but those piercing eyes were fastened on his face. It was as if his thoughts had summoned her.

Can the others see? She shook her head before he could even speak the words.

"My words are for you alone, Lord Sutcliffe."

"Why am I here?" he demanded, lowering his voice to a rumble as he entered the room. He tried to focus on the Sorceress, but her image kept wavering, like a reflection in moving water, floating a few inches above the floor.

"I thought you might benefit from a little trick I used with one of my other projects. Although the Maclean was invisible for far longer than you will be, Aiden. Neither of us has the time to dillydally, I'm afraid. Stewart is on his way, and there is much work to be done."

"Darlington was here," he said. "What of Lorne? Are he and Maggie safe?"

"You will know the answers to those questions when you need to know them, Aiden. At this moment you must form a bond with red headed Ally. She is your way forward, both with Stewart and your own journey. Open up to her."

"Blast it, woman, I need to find the others!" His voice had risen and for a moment he thought the knitting women would come rushing in, demanding to know who was there. He pushed the door closed with his shoulder and held it shut, just in case. He lowered his voice, but it was no less passionate. "You want me to do this now, when all of our lives are at stake? How can bonding with this woman be more important than saving my friends?"

She smiled and, apart from it making him feel shaky, he wanted to groan with frustration. "I like this new Aiden," she said. "You're arguing with me. You're not standing to one side and letting the situation wash over you. You're fighting to win."

"You know I'm not that man anymore," he said. "I've changed. Please, let me go to the others. Let me help them catch Stewart. Whatever you want from me can wait."

For a moment, he thought she was going to concede. That he had reached whatever passed for a heart behind that cold, inhuman exterior. He should have known better.

"Speak with Ally," she said. The humour was gone from her brilliant blue eyes. "Nothing here is a coincidence, Aiden. Everything is as it should be. Remember that. Everything happens for a reason, and she is the key."

He stared back at her, unable to move, unable

to resist her gaze, aware of his spinning head and wildly beating heart... and then she was gone.

Aiden leaned against the wall, gulping in air, trying to calm himself. Everything happens for a reason? Did that mean the Sorceress was going to be here with them, ready to help, ready to take Stewart when they captured him? She had been missing for so long and now she was back, and although he was confused and anxious, he was also relieved. Knowing she was here on Moyle was a relief.

If only he could tell the others.

Chapter Six

THE CREATURE CALLED Stewart, once known as Noakes, closed his eyes and smiled to himself. He had planned this for so long. Centuries. Every detail had been documented in his mind, then ticked off when it came to pass, or altered whenever the Marquis caused his plans to go awry.

The Marquis.

Charles Escott, the Marquis of Lorne.

The man was a foul stain upon humanity, and Stewart was going to remove him. It would be easier to swat him like a fly and toss the remains away, but that was too quick and easy. No, Lorne had to suffer, just as he had suffered. He had to ache and beg and weep until he was satisfied. Only then, in his graciousness, would he allow the man to die.

He'd had a taste of what was possible at Blackfriars Abbey, when Maggie McNab had been taken from Lorne and sent back to the past to see for herself what kind of a man the Marquis really was. Unfortunately, the stupid woman had decided she still loved him.

One could rarely rely on women to do the rational thing, Stewart thought with a grimace. Anyone else would have run screaming when they saw the type of man they were sharing a bed with.

He made a disgruntled noise and opened his eyes. There was nothing much to see. He was hidden away, awaiting the moment when he would make his appearance on Moyle. Hidden right under the Dark Lord's nose. The fool Zany had helped with that, in return for some special favours. The little creature had been very useful to Stewart, and seemed to enjoy playing his master off against that stupid Sorceress.

They would all be sorry soon, and he couldn't wait. He was going to enjoy the expressions on their faces when they knew at last that it was he who had bested them. That he was now in charge of all the worlds and could reshape them as he wished. Who would have thought the snivelling little bastard Noakes should rise so high?

Oh yes, he was going to enjoy his triumph. He truly was.

Chapter Seven

———◆———

L AUGHTER CAME FROM elsewhere in the cottage. Aiden relaxed when he realised that no one had come to see what the noise was. No one had heard him speak with the Sorceress. It was to be expected and no doubt there had been some magic involved. The witch wouldn't want to be seen by anyone other them him. She was devious like that. He'd heard she had transformed herself into an eagle to spy on others, though he had not actually seen it. But that had been the gossip when he was sheltering in the between-worlds, after the Hellfire Club's run in with Stewart at Lorne's ancestral home, and he had no cause to doubt it.

He glanced about. He was in Ally's bedchamber now… Bedroom, he reminded himself. Some knitted clothing was folded on the bed, and several boxes were stacked under the window. Something solid rested against the wall with a sheet-like cloth draped over it. Even knowing he shouldn't, Aiden crouched down and pulled the cloth aside. There was a looking glass, a mirror of sorts in a fancy frame. The surface was black, like polished metal, which seemed odd. Why had Ally covered it up?

Aiden let the cloth drop back into place. He couldn't hide here any longer. What if she discovered him and thought he was rummaging through her personal belongings? He went to open the door, being as quiet as he could, and followed the sound of the laughing women.

It seemed as though they were packing up. He stood out of the way and watched as they tugged on their coats and tied their hoods around their faces. There were some last-minute instructions and excited farewells, and then they were gone. When the last of them had stepped out of the cottage and into the squally rain, Alison closed the door and gave a deep sigh.

For some naive reason, Aiden had not expected it to be so inclement here. The photographs he'd seen of Moyle in Simon Frazer's book made the place seem idyllic. Of course, they were taken in summer, and this was most certainly not summer. It was probably impossible to hold a camera steady in the winter.

His thoughts turned back to Ally. What was he meant to do now? And how was Ally the key to all of this? As with most of the witch's pronouncements, this was a riddle. He wanted to push his way through the barrier that kept him in the cottage and escape, but he knew he was trapped. There was only one way out, and that was to do as the witch said. Persuade Ally to his side. Open up.

Ally's cut-glass accent interrupted his unhappy

thoughts. "Are you here?"

She seemed uncomfortable, and he supposed it must be a bit odd talking to an empty room. Although she had apparently sensed dead people all her life, so maybe their present circumstance wasn't quite so strange to her.

"Aiden?" Her voice softened. "Did all our prattling frighten you off? Or have you fallen into a coma out of boredom?"

He cleared his throat and her gaze locked in on him. "Still here."

Her mouth twitched as if she wanted to smile but was trying not to. "Have you tried to leave?" she asked. "I mean, to walk away from the cottage?"

"I tried when Nicholas and Linny were here. Something prevented it. A sort of wall... slimy and wet, yet invisible." He sought to find words for the disgusting barrier he had encountered, but gave up. "I couldn't get through," he admitted irritably.

She looked thoughtful for a moment. "Why do you think you're trapped here on Moyle?" she asked. "You mentioned a Sorceress...?"

"She has made me a prisoner," he grumbled. "She wants me here because..." He didn't want to tell her what the Sorceress had said, not until he understood better who this woman was and why she was suddenly so important to their quest. "Let us say her ways are mysterious."

"A prisoner?" Ally raised her brows. "Why would she do that?"

Aiden huffed. "God, where do I start?"

She laughed in surprise, her face lighting up, and warmth flooded his chest. "I find the beginning is always a good place," she said. Her face was turned to his, open and accepting, her eyes the colour of greengages. How would she react to the foolish things he and his friends had done in the Hellfire Club? He didn't wish to disgust her. He was beginning to like her and seeing her with the other women had allowed him to recognise a kindness within her. He didn't want her to think he was taking advantage of her.

At the same time, he and his friends were in desperate straits. Stewart would come for them soon and they needed to be ready, all of them. If she despised him for what he once was, then he would have to swallow that pain down. He had to do as the Sorceress demanded whether he wanted to or not.

She sensed his hesitation. "Please, you never know, it might help. I have guided lost souls to safety before."

Was he a lost soul? Perhaps he was. He looked into her pretty face, and something inside him shifted. He wasn't sure what it meant, but he had an urgent need to free himself of his burdens, lay them at her feet, and beg for her help.

"As you wish. I will start at the beginning." He took a deep breath. "My two friends and I formed a Hellfire Club. It was silly stuff, really, childish. An excuse to dress up, drink too much, and invite the prettiest women in the village to join us. A way for bored gentlemen to pass the time."

She looked amused, but there was also a frown between her arched eyebrows. "So you were a wealthy gentleman with too much time on your hands? I've read about those clubs. My father…" She stopped, as if something had occurred to her, then gave an awkward shrug. "It is exciting for a little while and then everyone gets bored and goes home. Is that what you did?"

"I wish we had," he said. "I wish…" He stopped because there was no point in regretting what had not happened, would never happen. Ally did not need excuses; she needed the truth. "No. We got bored and did something terrible. We called up a demon from the underworld and set it free."

She didn't laugh in disbelief. Her face went blank and her green eyes widened in shock. "You set it free?" she repeated in a whisper.

"We did not believe it would work, but that cannot excuse the fact that it did."

"I am assuming that didn't go well?"

"It went very badly indeed. The demon was called the Destroyer, and for good reason. It killed people. Far too many. It would have killed more, but we were able to capture it. Then the Sorceress dealt with it in the only way she could at the time. She sent it into a deep sleep, then she sent us to sleep as well, in case the Destroyer was ever awoken."

He went on to tell her how Maggie had accidentally brought the demon out of its sleep while working on an archaeological dig near Blackfriars Abbey, Lorne's ancestral home. How Lorne had been awoken, followed by Nicholas and himself, and they had managed to recapture the creature, only to learn there was much worse to follow. Stewart had been waiting, rubbing his hands together like the evil mastermind he was.

"Stewart wants to destroy us all, but it's Lorne he truly hates. When Lorne was growing up, the person who loved him the most was his nanny, Mrs Noakes. She was Stewart's mother, and he believes Lorne received all the affection that rightly belonged to him. I believe that is what it all comes down to. Envy and jealousy.

"The last time we encountered Stewart, he did his best to make Lorne suffer, but it backfired. We took Stewart prisoner, only to have to let him go in order to save Maggie's sister from the Destroyer. Now Stewart has led us here and he will not be satisfied until Lorne is in utter torment. To do that, he will bring down the whole of mankind… unless we stop him."

Her green eyes widened. "The end of days," she whispered.

"I suppose that's one way of putting it."

She stood, staring into thin air. Well, at him, Aiden supposed, but he didn't think she was looking outward. She was looking inside herself. She shook her head abruptly, as if to clear her mind of whatever thoughts consumed her.

With a sigh, she looked about her at the garments she and the other women had been working on. "I can't just drop what I'm doing," she said, and he suspected she spoke to herself. "I mean, if we're all going to die, then it doesn't matter whether we finish them or not, but everyone has worked so hard. And who am I to say what is or isn't important?"

Aiden wasn't quite sure how to answer that, although he preferred to take a positive slant. "My hope is we are not all going to die," he said. "My hope is that my friends and I will stop Stewart, hand him over to the Sorceress, and be allowed to go on our merry way."

He could see that he had startled her out of some dark thoughts. She was about to answer him when he heard a pitiful meow from outside.

"Oh God, Wayward!" she cried, and hurried to open the door.

A bedraggled black cat ran inside, then froze, staring at the spot where Aiden stood. Before it could flee outside again, Alison slammed the door and stood in front of it. The cat hissed and ran up the bookcase, observing them from its roost with its malevolent yellow eyes.

"She's terrified of your dog," Alison said, "and she's terrified of you. But don't let that worry you, she's also terrified of the knitting group." She sighed. "I'll feed her. That will get her down."

Aiden eyed the animal uneasily. "What did you call her?" The cat could see him, he was sure of it, and its claws looked sharp.

"Wayward. It's what the witches in Macbeth were known as. The Wayward Sisters. You know, 'Double, double, toil and trouble'?"

"Vaguely. Why Macbeth?"

"Because I'm in Scotland and... I don't know, it just seemed appropriate. She's a very mysterious cat, slinking around, popping up when I least expect her. And just look at her." She smiled up at the sulking animal. "You can imagine her laying curses on you, can't you?"

He laughed. It was probably the first time he had been amused enough to laugh since this business on Moyle began. "Indeed I can."

Aiden watched as Alison bustled around, finding a dish and filling it with dry cat food, then coaxing the cat into the kitchen. Wayward was quick to decide food was worth any risk, and began to gobble the kibble while Ally stroked her.

Although Ally spoke soothing words to her cat, it was clear something was bothering her. He noticed it in her pensive expression. He wouldn't be surprised if she was having second thoughts about having him in her house after what he had told her.

Maggie had accepted Lorne's story when they first met, but only because she had seen a demon with her own eyes. And Linny had been possessed by one of Stewart's demons. She had kept well away from the Hellfire Club boys because of that, and had only turned to them when she had no other choice.

But Ally had no reason to believe him. Just because she spoke with the dead did not mean she could not be sceptical. He had no proof of his story. In fact, she had every reason to keep her distance.

And yet there was something…

The end of days.

His stomach gave a loud rumble. Ally looked in

his direction and laughed. "Are you hungry? Of course you are. I have to keep reminding myself you're not exactly a ghost. Have you eaten at all since you got here?"

"I did take a slice of your pie from last night. And the oatcakes in the tin with some butter and cheese," he admitted, uneasy with the theft. "But nothing since then."

"I'll find you something. It's time for supper, anyway. And I need a break from this," she gave a wave of her hand to the colourful woollen garments. "There is still a bit to do before the ceilidh, but I think we'll manage."

"Will there be many there? At the ceilidh?" he asked, glancing out the window. "I wouldn't have thought the population of Moyle would be very large."

"You're right, it's not. It's mainly for the outsiders. It's going to be a popular event, and the owner of the island has done a good job of publicising it this year. And the outsiders, well, let's say they have deep pockets," she added with a grin. "I want their money."

Aiden chuckled.

She stared in his direction a moment, as if she wanted to say something important, and sighed instead. "Come and sit down," she said. "Mutton stew all right? I'm afraid we don't go in for anything too upmarket here on Moyle. I should add that the hotel does have some very nice haute cuisine, but few of the islanders can afford to go there."

"Mutton stew sounds perfect," he said as his stomach gave another groan. She laughed, and he felt absurdly pleased with himself.

Chapter Eight

ALLY HEATED THE stew, cutting slices of homemade bread and lathing them with farm butter. One thing about living on Moyle, despite the cost of importing some goods from the mainland, the food here was always fresh and delicious. Was it any wonder she had put on a few pounds?

Aiden Sutcliffe's story had been both bizarre and terrifying. The three friends acting so stupidly and reprehensibly, the Sorceress forcing them to make amends for what they had done, the long sleep, and then awakening into a strange new world. It sounded like something out of a fantasy novel.

Did she believe him?

If Ally had been an ordinary woman with an ordinary family from an ordinary life, she might have struggled with the idea. But she wasn't. She could speak with ghosts and help them adjust or move on. She had been told since she was young that she would be the catalyst for the end of mankind. These were not ordinary things.

But this was different. She needed convincing.

What was more, his words brought back a memory she had pushed far into the depths of her mind. It happened after she had left home. One night in her flat she had awoken suddenly to the feeling that she was not alone. Not unusual for ghost whisperer Ally, but the voice that had come out of the dark, croaky and so very old, was not the normal bewildered soul seeking the light. This ghost did not want her help, it had wanted to warn her.

"Beware, my lady. Beware of the man with many faces. He wishes to cause calamity through you. He wishes to bring on the end of times through you. Take care, my lady, take great care. Another man will come, a dead man who lives. He is your friend. Only through joining with him can you survive."

Ally had sat up, staring wide eyed into the dark. "What do you want from me?"

"I'm here to warn you, my lady. You have the capacity to do great evil, or great good. The one I love most will need you, and you must be ready."

It hadn't made much sense, but it was so strange that Ally had not forgotten.

Aiden wasn't the man with many faces, but he was a dead man who lived. He seemed very down to earth for someone who had so much baggage. And strange as it was, it felt as if there was something familiar about his story. As if both of them held different pieces of the same big puzzle. Perhaps together they might be able to complete it.

So she supposed she believed him, yes, but did she trust him? That was the sticking point, because she couldn't tell him about her past unless she did.

At the moment, despite everything, Ally was still on the fence about that. She didn't trust many people, with good reason, and an invisible rogue from the 1800s was the least dependable individual she could have chosen to put her faith in. Was a warning from a ghost in the night enough to set aside a lifetime's worth of caution?

She needed to think, yet she had the feeling that time was running out.

"Ready," she called out, and began to set the food on the table.

"I am here."

She smiled. Her invisible companion's chair shifted slightly as he took his place. He must be starving, living on pie and oatcakes. She'd given Loki the first bowlful of stew, having until now been feeding him with cat food, but she hadn't realised Aiden had been waiting here patiently until she heard him speak.

Now the dog sat on the floor at where she assumed Aiden's feet were. When she had let Loki out a little while ago, he had bounded from the laundry, moaning in ecstasy. Ally had watched as he was petted and rubbed by invisible hands.

Wayward had hissed furiously and returned to her sanctuary on top of the bookshelf.

"I don't think she wants to be your friend, Loki," Aiden had said, his voice deep and warm with amusement.

Wayward had given the dog a baleful look while Loki obviously would have loved to make the cat's acquaintance. But Wayward wasn't going to take any chances, and neither was Ally.

Now Loki was at his master's feet, having finished his helping of mutton stew. Ally poured a glass of red wine and passed it to him. She watched in amazement as it rose into the air and drained into nothing, disappearing the moment it passed his lips. This invisible stuff was disconcerting to say the least, but it was preferable to the alternative of actually seeing what he ate and drank be digested.

"Thank you," he said in that deep, aristocrat voice. "I am most grateful, Miss MacDonald-Ellis."

Ally stared at him in a bemused manner. "Please, Ally will do. Unless you want me to call you 'Mr Sutcliffe.'"

"Lord Sutcliffe," he said automatically, and then caught his breath.

"Lord Sutcliffe," she repeated, staring where she thought he was. "Well, I am a lady, or I could be if I wanted to be. My father is an earl. But I don't believe in all of that bollocks, and I have certainly never made an issue of it."

"I have not called myself Lord Sutcliffe for two hundred years." Then, with a surprised note in his voice, he asked, "Why don't you make an issue of it? Wouldn't your life be easier if you were known by your title?"

Ally supposed that might be the case in some quarters, but her life had always been very simple. In her younger years, she had been a bit of a radical, and she doubted some of her friends would have spoken to her at all if they knew she was aristocracy. She had been in the habit of ignoring her blue blood. Now, here she was, sharing her home with an invisible lord.

"Not for me," she answered at last. "I want to be anonymous."

"Invisible?" he asked dryly.

She smiled. "Not quite that anonymous, but I don't want to be caught up in that sort of world. I have my reasons." She said this firmly, letting him know without saying out loud that the subject was closed. For now, at least.

Night had fallen, and she could hear the wind moan around the cottage, tugging at the loose slate on the roof.

"At least you have a choice," Aiden said, and although she heard his despondency, she refused to be drawn into asking about it. There were secrets that needed to be shared, but not yet. She needed time to think, to make a decision.

"Perhaps by tomorrow things will make more sense," she said, partly to herself.

They ate in silence for a moment before he answered. "I cannot wait too long. Stewart is coming to Moyle, and I need to be with my friends when the curtain lifts on his grand finale. I need them, and they need me."

"I tried the phone again, there's still no signal. If you could get through this barrier you mentioned, maybe you could get to the town, but…" With a wave of her hand toward the windows, "The weather is pretty atrocious."

He gave that deep, rumbling laugh again. "I

should tell you about the between-worlds. That's pretty atrocious. At least on Moyle there aren't any loch horses or dragons, the sort of pets the Sorceress keeps in her realm."

Ally wasn't sure what to say to that. The images his words brought to mind were creepy, to say the least.

"Well," she said, taking a breath, "the island is full of myths and legends. I'm not sure if any of them are true, but I have a healthy respect for the supernatural for obvious reasons. The blue men, for instance. They have always given me a shiver, despite never having seen one."

"Blue men?" he asked. She heard the chair creak as he moved, shifting closer, and then the warm sensation of his body as he leaned against her. She stared at the empty space opposite her, willing herself to 'see' him, but there was noth- ing. It was as if something was blocking her from using her abilities. The ghosts who sought her out were not always easily seen, but there was usually something to distinguish them from their surroundings. A wavering light or a blurred fig- ure or a silhouette. And other times they were just like normal, living human beings. But with Aiden, she could see nothing, even though he was physically there.

"Yes, I've done a bit of research on them. They are busiest in winter. The blue men can conjure up storms, rather like tonight. They live in the waters around the islands, and they sink ships and drown sailors. In the summer, they sleep on the beaches or float in the calm waters. There have been historic reports of them being seen in these parts, all last century and earlier, nothing more recent. The general conclusion is that people probably saw seals or basking whales and only believed they were blue men."

"Sounds like something the Sorceress might want to add to her menagerie," he said with a trace of humour.

"Sometimes, when I walk on the beach, I look out at the water and try to see a blue man. No luck so far," she said with a smile. "I don't know what I'd do if I did see one. Get as far away from the water as possible, I expect."

Loki gave a big yawn, and Ally laughed. "I think your dog is trying to tell you something." She yawned and stretched herself, fighting another laugh. "It's late, and I'm tired. We'll see what tomorrow brings."

"I suppose I have no choice."

"You can sleep in the second bedroom. It's small, but it's all I have other than the sofa, and believe me, that is very uncomfortable. A friend slept there once when he stayed overnight and his back still hasn't recovered."

She led the way as she spoke and could hear Aiden's steps behind her, while Loki gambled all about them. She showed him the room and pointed out the extra blankets. He probably knew where everything was, he must have done a bit of exploring, but it served to fill what suddenly felt like an awkward silence.

Did she trust him? She had a large invisible man living in her cottage, one who had been part of a Hellfire Club and had helped bring a demon into the world because he was bored. And yet she considered herself a good judge of character, and Aiden Sutcliffe did not raise any red flags with her.

She liked him. There, she'd admitted it.

"Goodnight then," she said quietly.

"Goodnight," he replied as she closed the door.

Chapter Nine

———◆———

LORNE LAY IN the bed next to Maggie, staring into the darkness. The blinds were covering the windows, but the muffled sounds of the storm outside had kept him from sleep. Beside him, Maggie breathed softly, her warm body tucked against his. Lorne's love for her had grown beyond anything he could once have imagined, but such deep love came at a price.

Happiness might be fleeting, he told himself, but it was worth any pain that came next. He knew the moment he must leave Maggie was getting close. The Sorceress had warned him what to expect, and he had accepted the burden she had placed upon his shoulders, but that didn't make the knowledge any easier to bear.

His dearest love, the mother of his unborn child, would be left behind because he would have to face the consequences of his actions. The fact that he was a different and better man now did not absolve him of what he had done.

This afternoon, after the plane had flown over the hotel, they had all waited for Stewart to make his grand entrance. False alarm. Nothing had happened. Now it was night. The hotel had fallen silent, and yet he could feel a growing tension in the air. Something was about to happen.

They needed to be vigilant. They needed to be ready. The problem was, they didn't know what they had to be ready for. Stewart had a terrible gift for misdirection, and they were well aware that he would use it to his best advantage. Which meant they likely wouldn't know what he was planning until they were in the thick of it.

Lorne's thoughts moved from one worry to another. Where was Aiden? The big man had vanished after the explosion and they urgently needed to find him. He refused to believe his friend was dead, but was it possible he was already in Stewart's clutches?

Lorne's thoughts tumbled around in his head, and he couldn't seem to stop them.

Then, just for a moment, the storm outside stilled, and he heard the soft sound of the television. It came from the lounge between the two bedrooms, rather like the suite they'd shared back in Glasgow. He suspected Nicholas Darlington was also awake.

Lorne slipped out of bed, careful to tuck the covers around Maggie's sleeping form, and made his way to the lounge, softly closing the bedroom door behind him.

The lounge was in darkness, lit only by the flicker of the screen. Nicholas was on the sofa, leaning forward and staring at the television. Its light played across his stern features and he didn't seem to notice Lorne.

Nicholas and Linny's arrival at the hotel had been a surprise, though a pleasant one—he and Maggie had feared that the others had not survived. The fact they had arrived all but holding hands had been more of a shock.

But when he gave it some thought, Lorne realised he wasn't all that surprised after all. From the moment Linny had pushed her way into Maggie's cottage, demanding to know where her sister was, he could tell that Nicholas had been smitten. Later, when Linny returned to her life in Glasgow, his attraction had only deepened. They had all seen it and wondered how things would end.

Since the pair had returned from the Dark World, it was obvious their relationship had deepened to the point where they were inseparable.

Lorne strolled closer. "Can't sleep?"

Nicholas looked up with a frown. "Neither can you, it would seem."

Lorne came to sit down on the corner of the sectional sofa. "I'm worried about Sutcliffe." And leaving Maggie and my baby forever, but best not to talk about that.

"Yes. We need him." Nicholas reached down and rubbed his leg. No doubt that was what had kept him awake, Lorne thought. The pain in Nicholas's leg was always present. And although he never complained, it must at times be quite excruciating.

Lorne leaned back with a sigh. "We do."

Nicholas moved awkwardly, turning to stare at him. "Do you think Stewart is here already? He could be, couldn't he? Who's to say Maggie isn't right and he's hiding on the island somewhere, biding his time? Laughing at us."

He sounded bitter, and Lorne waited a beat before answering. He knew enough of Nicholas to understand how far he had come from the man he'd once been. It was galling for them all to know they had worked so hard to become better men, only to find themselves unable to control their own destinies.

"Clever as he is, Stewart has always underestimated us. His jealousy and rage cloud his vision. We need to remember that and use it against him. Let him think he'll win; that will make him more complacent until we can turn the tables."

Nicholas closed his eyes and nodded. For a moment Lorne watched the TV screen without truly seeing it. A car rolled over and burst into flames, but the device no longer amazed him as it once did.

"We need to use our time to find Aiden and work on a plan. Besides," he hesitated. "I think that if he were near, I would be able to feel him. I don't."

Nicholas seemed to relax a little. "I agree. This time, we need to be one step ahead of him instead of the other way around."

"Yes."

The two men exchanged a long look, and then Nicholas fell back against the sofa, running his hands through his loose hair and holding it at his nape. There was a red bruise on his neck. Lorne tried not to smirk.

"Bed bugs?" he asked, pointing at his own neck.

"Then you have them too," Nicholas muttered, then chuckled.

Lorne laughed aloud, and the mood suddenly seemed much lighter. "We are sad cases, aren't we? Who would have thought the mighty Hell-fire Club would end up so... tame?"

"I think it comes from loving and being loved."

"I didn't know what either of those things meant two hundred years ago. Until I met Maggie." He grinned, and Nicholas nodded.

"We're not the men we were then. And you're right, I can't imagine living in a world without Linny."

They grew silent again. Outside, the wind moaned and something on the roof of the hotel rattled as if it were about to take flight. Out at sea, the waves crashed and surged. Earlier, Lorne had watched them overwhelm the small pier, completely enveloping it in white foam.

"Why is the witch never here when we need her," he said, more a statement than a question.

"After what I saw in the Dark World, I'm not sure the Sorceress is as invincible as I once believed."

He had spoken to Lorne at length about the Dark World, but words were often inadequate when it came to that place. "Does she even have her mind focussed on Stewart and recapturing him? She seemed consumed instead by this thing between her and Sigurd, and all the while Stewart was running circles around them both. I'm worried, Lorne."

Lorne was worried too, but it was his job to lift his friend's spirits, not dash them.

"We've done this before. We had Stewart in our grasp and only released him to save others. I believe that proves we have the ability to triumph over that piece of shit."

Nicholas snorted a laugh. "I suppose."

Lorne smiled and rose to his feet. "I'm going back to bed, and you should as well. Let's sleep while we can." And enjoy the company of our women while we can, he thought, though he didn't say it. He didn't need to. Nicholas already knew.

As he went back to the bedroom he felt a deep sense of foreboding. Despite what he had said earlier, he knew this may not end well. He may have to leave Maggie and his friends behind, or he may end up forever in the underworld.

Stewart would love that. He had hated Lorne since they were children, with a relentless loathing that nothing seemed to satisfy. The only thing that might satiate that man was Lorne being hurt beyond bearing, and yet still left living.

He had tried to hurt him through Maggie before. That had backfired, but this time he would be even more determined to succeed. Just as Lorne was even more determined to defeat him. He had more riding on his winning than Stewart. Love triumphing over hate.

It was a good thought, and one he desperately wanted to believe.

Chapter Ten

—◆—

AIDEN SIGHED AND turned onto his side. As predicted, the bed in Alison's spare room was too small. His feet dangled off the end and his head bumped the hard wall every time he tried to stretch out.

It wasn't a bed meant for sleeping in if you were a big man such as him.

The night grew still now. The storm had passed, or at least quietened down. He could hear the cat-shaped clock on the wall ticking, its tail moving back and forth, and its yellow eyes looking from one side to the other. It looked rather like Alison's cat Wayward, only far more friendly. He suspected the animal hated him almost as much as she hated Loki.

His faithful hound lay on a small space of floor beside Aiden, snoring softly. It seemed he'd worn himself out tearing at the laundry room door. Aiden had again promised to pay for any damage, but Ally had only given the dog a droll look before going to bed and closing her door.

She wasn't frightened of Aiden, and that was fortunate. He wouldn't have been surprised if she were. A woman alone with an invisible man. It sounded like the opening to one of those creepy movies he'd watched in Glasgow on the hotel television. The wondrous device had increased Aiden's knowledge of modern life by leaps and bounds. He wasn't sure if any of that knowledge was really of much use, but it certainly aided in conversation. He knew who RuPaul was, and he now understood some of the modern expressions that had once baffled him. Some days, he thought he could almost pass for a modern man. Almost.

Aiden turned over, muttering a curse as he banged his head on the wall once again.

Once he was reunited with the others, they would find Stewart and this nightmare would be over. They could get on with their lives.

Get on with his life.

It seemed to be a theme that followed him. And yet, what could his life in the modern world really consist of? If everything went as planned, if they were allowed to remain here, he would have his friends. But Lorne had Maggie now, and a child on the way, and Nicholas was clearly besotted with Linny. They would make their own futures, and although Aiden would always be welcome, he feared the distance between them would begin to grow. It was the way of the world. There would always be a bond between them, but they would move on, and that was how it should be.

But Aiden was alone, apart from Loki. Would he find someone to share his solitude? He thought of Ally and frowned, staring up at the dark ceiling. He barely knew her, he told himself, and yet there was already a bond between them. Something mysterious and indefinable.

He sighed and turned over, his eyelids finally heavy. Life as it used to be flickered behind them, like one of those black and white films he had watched late at night when he was alone in the hotel suite in Glasgow. They had been jerky, stilted, and rather naïve, but he had been fascinated by the expressions on the faces of the actors. White faces heavily made up with dark eyes…

He drifted at last into sleep.

He was back in the between-worlds.

Aiden recognised this place with a sense of dread. His steps slowed and stopped as he stared at the narrowing tunnel before him and its lowering roof. Seeing the confined space didn't inspire him to go any further… and yet there was a blue light up ahead, one he knew that meant the Sorceress was waiting for him. Again.

Hadn't one visit in the past few hours been enough? Were they running out of time? Was that the problem? The witch seemed to be determined to force him to spill his final secret before their confrontation with Stewart.

He had a choice. Push on through the shrinking tunnel, or turn back and wander for hours, looking for another way out.

Until he confronted her, he was unlikely to escape this place—and this dream—and he was very keen to do both. While he had slept in the pet cemetery at Blackfriars Abbey, he had had many such dreams. The witch had pummelled his head and heart endlessly, forcing him to face a past he wished to leave hidden. She had taken him apart piece by piece, and he had come to understand the reason why he was the man he was, how that past had shaped him. She had taught him how he might be better.

And he was better. He knew it, felt the change deep inside. He had learned the lessons of his past and could see with clear eyes how that past had brought about his own downfall. A small mistake here, a larger one there, they had all combined to cause him to fail himself and his friends at the most crucial of times.

He wouldn't make the same mistake again. He wouldn't.

But what was the point of making him a better man if the Sorceress was going to send him to the underworld after all this, or back to the past to be hanged by the local magistrate at best, slaughtered by an angry mob at worst?

"Because you can't escape justice, Aiden."

The voice shocked him into lifting his head, only for it to crack painfully against the rough roof of the tunnel.

"Ouch!" He rubbed the bruise and gawped at the creature standing before him. It didn't matter how often he saw her, she never failed to leave him speechless. She was enveloped by blue light, her red hair waving in a non-existent breeze, her eyes the colour of the ocean. A Caribbean ocean, such as those his father had sailed across when he visited the family estate in the West Indies.

He felt his gorge rise and swallowed heavily before he lost Ally's mutton stew.

"You don't look very happy, Lord Sutcliffe."

"I'll be happier when I get away from this place and find Lorne and Darlington. Where are they, madam?"

"You'll see them soon enough," she said comfortably, which only increased his frustration. "Are you thinking of your father, Aiden? You have that pinched look to your face that you get whenever you think of him. Are you wondering whether you inherited more from him than just your title?"

"I try not to. Think of him, I mean."

"You just did."

He cleared his throat, hoping she would leave it. But she wouldn't. She never did. He waited for her next assault on the locked door inside his chest. It had already cracked, and it was only a matter of time before it burst wide open.

"You know he is at the heart of all your problems. You are a far better man than he. Just because he sired you does not mean you must take the blame for his actions."

Logically, Aiden knew that, but part of him still believed those events from his past were his fault, and that fear had influenced his actions for years. He took a deep breath and fixed his eyes on the witch, though it made him uneasy to meet those electric blue orbs.

"We need your help, madam. To defeat Stewart, we need you with us."

She smirked. "I think you are perfectly capable of defeating him on your own. Deliver him to me, and I will do the rest."

She began to move away, though without walking, one of her unnerving tricks. "And Aiden," she called, as she grew fainter, "do listen to Ally. She is your companion in this. Help her, and she will help you. No man is an island, even when they are on one."

The watery blue light then abruptly blinked out, leaving him hunched over in the too small tunnel, alone in the dark.

He reached up and placed his palm on the ceiling, wincing at the sensation of rough stone and wet slime.

Just because he sired you does not mean you must take the blame…

The words tasted foul at the back of his throat. His father, big and loud, a man he had been drawn to just as everyone else had been drawn to him. Even when he learned the truth about the man, he couldn't help but love him, want his approval, need his attention.

Until one day he realised how dangerous and sick it was, following in the footsteps of a man whose actions he had come to loathe so deeply. How it was damaging him. How his father's evil stuck to him in ways he might never escape. And if he didn't want to end up exactly like him, he needed to turn his back on the man and walk away.

But that was much more difficult than it sounded, because it meant walking away from his inheritance, his title, and everything he was supposed to be.

And what then? Who would he be if he did that?

As if in answer, a torch behind him suddenly flared up. He couldn't help but chuckle. At least the witch wasn't going to keep him here forever. She was guiding him out of this infernal place.

Aiden turned and began to follow the light.

Chapter Eleven

ALLY WAS UP early, just as she always was. Even on cold and damp days like this, she was raring to go by the time dawn broke. It was one of the traits that had set her apart from the others in her father's commune, who had liked to sit up all night drinking and discussing their crazy beliefs, then sleep through to the afternoon.

Besides, her busy brain kept reminding her it was only two more days until the ceilidh! She needed to have all the garments finished by then, and she needed to set up shop in the hotel foyer.

She had planned everything down to the last detail, but something was bound to go wrong. Well, technically, it already had. She had an invisible man who was trying to stop the end of days living in her house…and his pet dog. But Ally still wanted to make this enterprise the absolute best it could be, because she had a lot riding on it. The whole island did.

When she had brought up the idea, the other women on the island had been sceptical, but now they were almost as excited as Ally. This could put Moyle on the map in a way that was far more culturally important than any ostentatious hotel.

Doubt now assailed her, curbing her excitement. Did she really want her new home on the map? Hadn't she come here so that she could disappear? But, she reminded herself, she could still be anonymous. There was no vanity riding on this. She and the other women were a collective, even their business name was nonspecific, Moyle Enterprises. It needed something catchier, she knew that, but so far a good name had eluded her. Well, she still had two days to think of one.

After she got dressed, she made her way to the kitchen to make a pot of tea. Coffee was expensive to bring to Moyle, but tea was abundant, so she had switched her drug of choice shortly after she arrived. The sky outside looked brighter now that the rain and wind had moved on. Not that it couldn't change again in a heartbeat.

She felt a nudge at her thigh. Loki looked up at her with hungry doggy eyes. She couldn't help but snort a laugh.

"I'll find you something in a moment," she said. "Go outside and do your thing first."

The dog went willingly enough, trotting out into the backyard. Perhaps Aiden had done the honours during the night, because Loki seemed more interested in nosing among the plants than squatting or lifting his leg.

She kept the door open and left him to it, then went to check her phone for a signal. Yes! It was working. Now Aiden could find where his friends were staying, though Ally would have taken money on it being the hotel in town. He still couldn't leave the cottage, but they should be able to come here. At least he would be one step closer to being reunited with them.

Eager to give him the good news, she hurried to the spare bedroom. The door was already ajar, which was how Loki had got out, but she heard only silence inside. Instead of stopping to knock, she pushed it wide open and peeped in.

There was a man lying on the bed.

She saw a broad naked back and dark messy hair. His face was buried in the pillows. He wore jeans, his long legs were stretched out, bare feet dangling off the end. After a second of startled confusion, her gaze lingered.

The muscles in his back were so defined, his wide shoulders leading to strong arms and his hands relaxed above his head. He was a big man, so everything was in proportion. She'd guessed he was big when she'd bumped into him, and when she sensed him close to her. Now she knew for certain. What did his face look like? For some reason, she had been thinking of David Gandy and it would be interesting to see how close she was.

Ally edged around the bed, trying to get a look at his face, most of which was still buried in the pillows. Strands of dark hair were tangled across his forehead, and she could see part of a cheek-bone and his nose, which seemed straight and long, and his parted lips, which looked firm and thin. As she bent down closer, he gave a soft snore and jerked. She gasped and stepped back, hitting the nightstand and making a sound.

Aiden's eyes popped open as his head shot up. They were as dark as his hair, the lashes long and lush. He squinted as if he thought he must have dreamt her.

Oh yes, he was handsome, though not the clean-cut, classical look of David Gandy. Aiden was more rugged than that. But she wasn't disappointed, not in the slightest.

Just then, Loki's large and hairy form sprang onto the bed, landing on Aiden's back, tail wagging and moaning. Ally let out a shriek and stumbled again, falling to the floor.

"Loki!" She pushed at the dog as it tried to leap from Aiden to her.

"Wha...?" Aiden's deep voice sounded confused. Then he roared, "Loki! Down!" and the dog dropped down to the floor, giving his master a sheepish look.

Aiden turned his head and peered at her, and seemed to catch something in her expression.

"You can see me." He pushed himself up, and he was close to her, looming over where she sat on the floor, gazing up at him. "You can see me!" he roared.

Loki started to howl.

Just for a moment, she experienced sensory overload. The sleepy masculine scent of him, the scruff on his jaw, those dark eyes staring down into hers, and the bulging muscles of his chest and arms, caging her in. It was too much for her.

He seemed to realise the problem, and shuffled back on the bed, still staring at her. His cheeks were flushed, his eyes bright, and he swallowed.

"You can see me," he repeated breathlessly.

"Yes, I can."

Loki came to give her a sniff, and she pushed the hairy face away before he could lick her too. Aiden reached out and grabbed the dog by the scruff of the neck and dragged him back. Loki looked as if his feelings had been hurt.

"Why? Why now?" Aiden asked.

"I don't know." Her gaze dropped and she stared at his chest, dark hairs growing in a patch between his nipples and down to his belly. Her eyes rose abruptly, and for a moment they stared at each other in silence. His mouth quirked at the corner.

"I don't know," she said it again, more firmly. "Really. I came to tell you that the mobile phone has a signal, and"—she gestured at his solid form wildly—"here you are."

His dark eyes gleamed as if there were a light behind them. "That's good, very good." He jumped up and held out his hand to her. After a moment, she took it, feeling the hard warm grip of his fingers as they closed over hers, and he tugged her to her feet with more exuberance than necessary. She gasped as she fell against him before she could steady herself.

His hands closed on her shoulders, making sure she had found her balance before he let her go.

"We must find Lorne and the others," he said as he strode toward the door. She watched him duck his head beneath the lintel. He was tall, very tall, and as big as she had imagined him. He was a remarkable specimen, as her knitting companions might coyly say.

She was still standing there when he ducked his head back in through the doorway. "Ally? The phone?"

Ally shook her wits back into place. "Yes, we'll ring them," she said. "Unless... do you think maybe you are able to leave the cottage now? Perhaps that has changed as well?"

He looked thoughtful, and then nodded. "Let us find out."

She followed him out to the doors that led onto the narrow terrace. The sun shone weakly through the overcast sky, but at least it was out. He was now halfway to the gate, Loki skipping excitedly at his side. Her eyes were glued to his naked back, the trim waist, and muscled buttocks beneath his tight jeans. He was a sight to behold, and she felt a bit lightheaded.

Ridiculous. It wasn't as if she hadn't seen a man naked before, and this one was half clothed. But there was just something about Aiden Sutcliffe that made her ridiculously swoony.

He pushed the gate open and took several steps forward, then stopped. It was the strangest thing. He came to an abrupt hold and made a sound, as if the air had been forced out of him, before he stumbled back.

"Bloody hell!" he growled, shaking his head and then giving an entire body shudder. If the matter hadn't been so serious, Ally might have laughed.

She approached him cautiously, looking beyond him to the empty space the mysterious wall was supposed to be. She took another step, and then another, but nothing impeded her progress, and soon she was beyond that point. She turned to face him.

He stared at her, hands on his hips. "You felt nothing?"

She shook her head, tucking a strand of auburn hair behind her ear. "Nothing." She walked back to him and they both turned and stared at the space. "Perhaps if we do it together?"

He seemed sceptical, but gave a nod. They had only gone a dozen steps when Aiden gasped and once more came to an abrupt halt, while Ally sailed through. At the last moment, she reached out to grasp his arm.

In that moment, he cried out and stumbled forward. Then he was with her, on the other side of whatever the obstruction had been. He dropped to one knee, panting as if he had run a race, staring up at her.

"I got through," he said in amazement.

"I think it happened when I touched you."

"We did it together." He seemed to be thinking hard, but whatever had occurred to him, he wasn't sharing it. "We can go to the hotel now," he said. "We don't have to ring."

"If you're sure." She looked up at the sky, scanning it for more bad weather, but the storm had gone for now. But Moyle weather was not to be trusted this time of year. There were sure to be more gales on the way.

"I am very sure," he said. There was a flush in his cheeks, and relief in his dark eyes. "Let's go."

Chapter Twelve

———◆———

THE BARRIER THAT had kept him from leaving the cottage had vanished! Aiden struggled to understand how something that had been so frustratingly impossible to conquer had suddenly turned so simple.

What had the witch told him? He and Ally must become a team; they must work together. He hadn't properly understood the Sorceress's words until now. If Ally could get him through the wall, then what else could they do? Could she help him defeat Stewart?

Surely not, but Ally must have hidden talents. It occurred to him that she was still a bit of a mystery. He had told her about his past, but she had said little about hers. He knew of her ability to see spirits, but what else could she do? Was she hiding something from him? He had trusted her instinctively from the moment he saw her, but should he?

Ally was watching him, and he wondered with a jolt how much of his mind she had read as these dark thoughts flitted through. Probably not much. Aiden had learned to wear his affable, friendly mask from an early age. Not many people knew the true man behind it.

"Did you know that would happen?" he asked her.

Her green eyes narrowed. "How could I? Do you think I go around holding hands with strange men all the time?"

Aiden's brow furrowed.

"It just… happened, that's all."

Some of his suspicions eased. "The Sorceress told me I must work with you," he admitted. "She said you were important to me. To us. That together, we could save the world. Do you know anything about that?"

"Did she?" Ally's gaze dropped, and he knew he was right. She did have secrets.

"There's something you're not telling me."

"Perhaps I don't want to tell you."

"And yet I trusted you with my story."

For a moment, he feared she would continue to refuse to share with him. "You're right," she admitted with a sigh. "There is something. You mentioned the end of the world. 'End of days'. I have heard that term before."

The hairs on his nape stood at attention. "Please, tell me," he said quietly.

"Not here. Inside."

———◆———

Alison took a breath. They were seated on the sofa, and she was about to tell him something she had not spoken of aloud for years. Something she kept locked away in her nightmares.

It would have been easier if he had still been invisible, she thought wryly, but she couldn't wish that on him again. Not when those dark eyes were so focussed on her, his expression so intent.

He was waiting.

"My father is Quentin Ellis, the Earl of Cleveland. My family made its fortune and was given its title during the wars around the time of Queen Anne. We haven't done much since then."

He nodded. "I know of them, but the Sutcliffes were not intimate with them." Again he waited.

"Oh. Well, I'm sure you haven't heard of my father, but most people have. At least the generation that was around in the 1960s. Free love. Mods. The Beatles. All that."

Once more he nodded, but she couldn't tell whether he had recognised any of those things. Aiden Sutcliffe wore a mask, she realised. He might seem easy going, with a ready smile, but he had unexplored depths. Not all of which he wanted to share.

"My father inherited the family estate and all the money he could possibly want. Some people would have spent their time jet setting around the world to celebrity parties. Others might have become philanthropists or businessmen, or country gentlemen striding around in their wellies. My father started a commune."

"A commune?"

"Sort of a place where everyone shares everything. He was a product of the times, and that meant experimentation with drugs, broadening his mind, rejecting social norms, and throwing off the shackles of a restrictive society." She checked to see if he was following her, thinking that such concepts were probably beyond his experience. But instead of looking puzzled, he smirked.

"Sounds rather like the Hellfire Club," he said. "We pretended we were broadening our minds and defying the restrictions of civilised society, but the truth was we were privileged and bored, and most of the time we just wanted to escape. I probably have a bit in common with your father."

Ally suddenly pictured Aiden dressed up in some outlandish costume, wielding a whip, and just as quickly pushed the thought aside. This man seemed far too, well, 'sane' to have done anything so ridiculous. But then she remembered some of the people her father surrounded himself with. Anyone could get drawn into that sort of lifestyle. Addiction, power, love, boredom. There were plenty of reasons a person might choose to remain in a place that was obviously bad for them. She knew that all too well.

"I take it your father did not call up demons from hell?" Aiden asked.

"No, but I'm sure he gave it a try once or twice. He surrounded himself with religious freaks and various gurus, plus all their hangers on. I remember one who claimed that by sleeping with him, you would be lifted to a higher level of consciousness. It was utter crap, but people will believe anything if they want to. And there were lots of drugs, endless tubs of booze, and sex. Lots of sex. The parties went on all night, and then everyone slept most of the day. There was no need to go to work or home, wherever that may have been, because Dad supplied them with everything they wanted."

"Again, this sounds much like the Hellfire Club," he said dryly. "Not the drugs, but red wine, yes, and the insane ideas. And the sex. Sometimes we'd be down in the crypt for days, completely off our faces. I can't remember most of what went on then, and I suppose I'm rather glad of that. These days I feel ashamed of the man I once was."

Ally stared at him, struck by the thought that she had met a man who truly understood what she was talking about.

"Is 'off our faces' the correct term?" he asked with a frown. "Sometimes I don't manage to get these modern idioms quite right."

"It's exactly right," she assured him. "They were living a different life to the world around them, a place where they believed they were cleverer than anyone else. Why get bogged down in a nine to five job with a wife and children and all the responsibility that entails, when you can do whatever you like and be told that it is the universe's plan for you? That you are somehow better than anyone else?"

"Until a demon from hell shows you what a fool you truly are," he muttered. "We all have to grow up, eventually, Ally. Some of us are simply more grown up to start with."

"My father has never grown up," she admitted. "Besides, it's too late now. I don't see him, haven't seen him for years."

"What about your mother?"

"She was one of the women who turned up with some of dad's friends, and caught his eye. An innocent Scottish girl who'd come for some excitement. Well, she got that all right. For a while she and my father were even exclusive, something that hadn't happened before. Perhaps it was her sweet innocence that made him fall for her. He told me that he loved her, and perhaps he did, but not enough to abandon his lifestyle."

"And how much was that lifestyle part of your life?"

"I didn't really take part when I was a child. Dad kept me away from the worst of it."

"Did your mother stay?"

"For a while. I haven't seen her in a long time now, but I've been told she got tired of the whole crazy situation and moved on."

"She didn't take you with her?"

Ally shook her head. "She left me there. I've thought about looking her up, or at least finding out what happened to her, but I haven't. I can't blame her for leaving, but if she really cared about what happened after she left, she would have done the looking up.

"Anyway, my father didn't encourage me whenever I spoke about her, and I suppose I just let it go. I had enough on my plate at the time, and I doubt she could have helped me. I got a sense from some of the others that she had been desperate to put it all behind her and just go home."

Ally wiped her palms down over her leggings. Her skin was damp with nerves and memories, and the worst was still to come. Best to get it over with.

"As I grew up, it wasn't as easy to keep me away from what was going on all around me. I was away at boarding school a lot of the time, but there were holidays when I came back home. A couple of times I stayed with friends or my aunt, but not always. So I heard things and saw things, and once in a while I had to be rescued from some of the more drugged out members of the commune. My father threw anyone who was a threat to me out on their ear, so that was something. I never doubted that he cared for me, and he didn't want me to join in with his crowd. He used to say that when I was older I could make my own choices, but until then, I had to keep my distance."

Aiden gave a nod of approval. "He kept you safe."

"He was protective. Then, when I turned eighteen, my father discovered a new guru, and everything changed. Things got a lot more edgy on the estate."

Aiden heard the grim note in her voice and leaned forward. "How so?"

"This guru knew I had unusual abilities. That I could see the dead, and that when I couldn't see them, I could still sense them."

"How did he learn of it?"

"I didn't exactly keep it a secret. I'm not sure when I realised how I was different from everyone else. When it started happening, I had help from one of the women at the commune who knew something about what I was going through. I was comfortable enough with my differences by then, though I never enjoyed being that way. And then this man came along and singled me out.

"He was charismatic. He had a way of making you feel as if you were the most important person in the room. When he spoke about his beliefs, a hush fell over his followers. Everyone believed him. Worshipped him, almost. And he wanted me to be part of his inner circle. He said I was important and he had to teach me how to rein in my abilities. He said if I didn't, there would be dire consequences for everyone. For the world. He spoke about the end of days, Aiden."

She saw the stillness in his expression, the tension in his broad shoulders.

"So you can imagine how I felt when you started talking about this Stewart person and saving the world," Ally said, taking a breath. "But it was worse than that, because this guru said that I was 'the one' who would bring about this end. That was why he wanted me restrained, under his power. He wanted to keep a close eye on me until I was ready to do whatever it was he wanted of me.

"The worst thing was, my father believed him. He began to look at me differently. Others did too. Then more people started joining the commune and they were even wackier. It was no longer somewhere I wanted to be anywhere near. So I left, ostensibly to go to university, but I never intended to go back."

"And your father let you leave? This guru let

you leave?"

"I was of age. They couldn't legally stop me. My father didn't realise I had no intention of coming home, so he had no reason to prevent me from going. And I think he felt a bit guilty for the way I had been treated by his new pet."

"So, what did you do next?"

"I was working on an arts degree in textiles and I kept my head down, but he still could have found me easily enough if he wanted to. After a couple of years, I heard that the end of days man had moved on. Maybe he realised the world wasn't ending, at least not just yet, or maybe he lost some credibility. Maybe he found someone else to wrap his tentacles around. I thought of him like that, an octopus, with tentacles everywhere."

"He didn't touch you, I hope?" Aiden asked.

Ally shook her head. That was one blessing, at least. The guru hadn't seemed interested in her sexually. It was her abilities he wanted and somehow that felt worse.

"You don't know what happened to him?"

She shook her head. "I was tempted to try and find him on the internet, but I was afraid to. I know it sounds ridiculous, but it felt as if searching for him would somehow draw his attention to me. I thought I saw him once, outside the building where I was living at the time, and it freaked me out. I wanted to stay away from him and not give him any reason to seek me out. My father was getting older, and things had quietened down at home. Honestly, I think that guy freaked him out as well. I still stayed away, though."

"Sounds like you did the right thing."

"Maybe. But my abilities were getting stronger, and I had no one to help me cope. Lost souls were turning up day and night. Everywhere I went, there were problems they wanted me to solve, and I was exhausted from trying to pretend nothing was happening while out in public. I decided to get as far away from people as I could. That's why I'm here on Moyle. And the thing is, since I've been here, I haven't had any spirits try to contact me. The dead are leaving me alone. It's as if there's some sort of barrier around Moyle, keeping me safe."

"So you don't believe you are the catalyst that will end the world?" he asked. "You don't believe what this guru said was the truth?"

"I don't want to. I don't understand how I could be that person. A twenty-eight year old woman who specialises in textiles and knitting? How can I possibly have anything to do with the end of days? Just because I can talk to the dead? It makes no sense."

"Yet here you are," he said, watching her. His dark eyes seemed to see a great deal—two hundred years of experience lay behind them.

"Yet here I am," she agreed.

Loki stretched on the floor at Aiden's feet and yawned loudly. It broke the awkward silence that had grown between them, and they both laughed.

"This man… this guru. What was his name?"

"Ari," she said. The name fell like a heavy stone in a pond, sending out ripples. Was this why the ancients did not say the names of those they feared? In case it brought them to their doors?

"Was he American?"

"No. Armenian, I think. At least, that was what I heard. Why do you ask?"

"I feel as if your story is linked to ours somehow. I need to talk to Lorne and Darlington. I need to talk to the Sorceress," he added irritably. "She's never around when I want her, only when it amuses her."

"Why do you believe our stories are linked? Do you think you were brought here because of me? That we were meant to connect?"

"The Sorceress believes so." He groaned and ran his hands down his face. "If only she would just explain what the hell is going on, but she makes us beg for every bloody drop of information."

Ally smiled. "Why does she make you beg?"

"She wants us to be better men. It's her way of teaching us a lesson."

"Oh? And do you think you have become better men?"

"Oh yes." There was something flirtatious in his smile. "Almost completely renewed."

Aiden Sutcliffe was a very appealing man, but it was best not to be drawn in by him. Their priority was to sort out what was happening on Moyle. A wave of concern swept over her. Her home was here, her friends too, and if anything happened to them because of her, then she would never forgive herself. This past year on the island had been the best year of her life... until now.

She would rather fall victim to the blue men than have anyone on Moyle hurt because of her.

Chapter Thirteen

ALLY WHEELED HER scooter out of the garage at the side of the cottage, although it was more of a shed than a garage. There wasn't room for a car in it, even if cars had been allowed on the island. The closest thing to a car here was a fleet of golf buggies the hotel rented out to visitors, although the locals used them too. But mostly it was either a walk or a bike if you wanted to get anywhere, or, in her case, a scooter.

The scooter was pink with chrome fittings, and very shiny. She had had it shipped over in a moment of madness after a few drinks with friends in a pub in Glasgow. A sort of farewell to her old life and hello to the new.

Walking to the small town that was the capital of Moyle would take too long, and besides, she would never keep up with Aiden's long legs or Loki's lope. This way, they would reach the hotel quicker and hopefully before any change in the weather.

Aiden stood, hands on hips, silently staring at the machine with a doubtful expression.

"I'm not sure I'll fit on this."

She met his gaze, noting that his doubt was mixed with amusement. Something inside her stilled at the sight. A lock of Aiden's hair fell into his eyes, and he raked it back with his long fingers. He stared at the scooter as if he could will it to increase its size. When she didn't answer him, he looked up and frowned.

"You can still see me?"

"Yes, I can still see you."

His expression brightened and he gestured at the scooter. "Are you sure about this?"

"Definitely. And yes, you will fit on the scooter. You'll just have to hold on to me. I'll go slow. Don't worry, you won't fall off."

"I'm more comfortable on a horse."

She laughed. "No horses here, only horse-power."

She thought that had gone over his head until he answered and she realised he'd been musing. "Maggie tried to teach me to drive. I was better at it than Nicholas, but that is not saying much. Perhaps I could drive your scooter."

"Perhaps. Not today, though. Come on, climb on."

"What about Loki?"

They could hear the dog's protests coming from the cottage. Alison shuddered to think of Wayward trapped on top of the bookshelves like a prisoner.

"He'll destroy your house," Aiden added.

With a sigh, Ally nodded, and Aiden strode back to the cottage. Soon after, Loki appeared, leaping and bouncing, eager to be a part of whatever adventure they were about to embark upon. She doubted the beast would have any trouble keeping up with them.

Mounting the scooter was probably the most difficult part. After some initial missteps in which Aiden nearly toppled off, they set out. Ally told him repeatedly to hold on to her, which he seemed reluctant to do. Perhaps it was an old-fashioned thing—riding a motor scooter behind a woman was not something Mr Darcy had ever had to deal with in Pride and Prejudice.

Eventually he did as she asked, and Ally tried to ignore her intense awareness of the heat she felt being so close to him. His strong arms were wrapped around her waist, and her bottom was tucked into the v of his thighs. She realised it had been a long time since she had been held by a man.

She'd had boyfriends; of course she had. She was twenty-eight years old. Just not many. After she had left home, she had wanted to concentrate on her studies, and she had been cautious when it came to letting people into her life. As time went on, she began to relax, began to believe the past was just that. She pushed the fear Ari had put into her out of her head.

It was crap after all, wasn't it? She had told a few close friends about her childhood on the commune, although she'd kept the 'end of days' part to herself. They had expressed disbelief that there were still people in the world who believed in that rubbish. Ally had laughed when they did, and rolled her eyes for good measure. It was good to make fun of her past; it helped take away its power over her.

But boyfriends were usually short term. They said she was closed off, secretive, and that much was true. She rarely shared more than the super-ficial with them, so they soon drifted away, found someone else, moved on. And so did she.

And now she had shared with Aiden Sutcliffe corners of her life she had never spoken of before. And he had listened and understood. She was still coming to terms with that. He hadn't laughed or sneered or told her it was all nonsense. Well, how could he? His own story was even weirder than hers.

She drove down the track that led to town, Loki loping beside them, glad to be free. She pushed her thoughts aside to concentrate on keeping them from slipping on the wet surface. Some parts of the path were more dangerous than others, so she took care. Slowing down at the corners, being cautious to stay on the higher side of the track. The storm may have passed, but Ally knew there was always another one brewing this time of the year.

Aiden remained quiet. Occasionally his arms would tighten when they turned a corner, then loosen again. His big, hard body enclosed hers in a way that should have made her nervous, but instead she found it oddly comforting. She trusted him, which should have surprised her, but didn't.

They were travelling along the shore now, the beach a long pale line between the sandy hillocks and the slate sea. The storm waves had thrown up seaweed, as well as flotsam tossed overboard from the ferries and other boats that plied these waterways. There were dead fish too, and the sea birds were there feasting on them. Further out to sea, the waves still surged but the white horses had gone. Everything was calm, at least for now.

Loki took a sudden turn and raced down onto the beach. Until now, he'd either been running alongside them or a bit ahead, with occasional stops to look back and wait for them to catch up. She heard Aiden chuckle as the dog approached the waves cautiously, only to jump back whenever a foam tipped surge slid toward him.

"Hasn't he ever seen the sea?" she asked above the sound of the motor. She tried to turn her head to see his face, but the wind blew her hair into her eyes. She had tied it back in a ponytail, but strands kept escaping. Aiden tried to tuck a strand back into place, making her start.

"As nice as it might taste, you probably don't want me eating your hair, Ally."

Ally tried not to let herself melt at that deep, soft voice. God, was she really so pathetic that one handsome man could have this effect on her? But Aiden was more than just a man, wasn't he? The way that he understood her life, it felt sometimes as if he were her other half.

Just then, Loki began to howl. Aiden's arms tightened about her so that the scooter swayed to one side. "Stop!"

She pulled over, a bit breathless from the squeeze. "What is it?"

But he was already off the scooter and running over the tussocks of grass that covered the small sand hills above the beach, down in Loki's direction.

The dog was near a mass of kelp, just above the waterline, making some dreadful noises. Alison turned off the motor and dropped the kickstand, then took off after Aiden.

At first, she could see nothing. Loki danced about, growling, howling, darting back and forth. There was clearly something in the kelp he didn't like. She could only think it might be an injured seal or a large fish. Aiden stopped abruptly and reached out to his dog, dragging Loki to heel and holding the animal as it struggled to get free.

"What is it?" Ally shouted as she reached them.

Aiden's gaze was fixed on whatever lay among the slimy kelp leaves. "Keep back," he warned her. "It's caught up in a fishing net, but look at those claws."

Cautiously, she stepped closer, and that was when she saw it.

Something that resembled a man was tangled in an abandoned fishing net. A hand reached out, and she saw the claws Aiden had warned her about, long and hooked. His fingers were webbed. Was the creature covered in oil? Because it was coloured blue, a very dark blue.

He—she just assumed it was a he—made a moaning noise, then a hiss that went on and on. Ally shivered. The creature turned to her. Blue irises surrounded by pure white stared up at her, and something in those strange eyes tugged at her heart. There was anger there, but also fear and desperation.

Help me, he seemed to say, the words echoing inside her head.

"What sort of creature is it?" Aiden asked.

Loki squirmed, wanting to get at the creature, but Aiden held him firm.

"I think he's a storm kelpie," she said, still staring at the creature.

Aiden turned to look at her. "Do you mean a demon?"

"Not a demon. A blue man. I told you about them." She kept her voice low and calm, not wanting to frighten the creature any more than it already was. "Island myths and legends are full of them, but I've never seen one. The blue men are known in the winter for calling up storms and gales to sink ships and drown sailors."

"Sounds like a demon to me."

The dog gave a long, desperate howl.

"Loki!" Aiden roared, catching him around the muzzle and holding him firm. "What should we do?" He turned to Ally once the dog had quietened. "I don't mean to sound uncaring, but they don't sound harmless to me."

"He won't hurt us," Ally said. "He just wants to go home."

Aiden stared at her, his dark eyes narrowed with distrust. "How do you know?"

She shrugged. "I can feel it."

He stared at her a moment longer, weighing her words, and she wondered if he was going to refuse to believe her. Then he gave a reluctant nod. "Very well. Do you have anything to cut the net? We should still keep away from those claws."

Ally reached into her bag and took out the pocketknife she always carried with her. It came in handy for the serious business of cutting a sheep—they ran free on the island—from a thorn bush, or collecting heather for the cottage.

Aiden gave a huff of laughter. "Indeed, you are a woman who is prepared for anything," he said. There was a gleam of admiration in his eyes. "Do you want me to attend to the creature? You'd have to hold Loki."

She shook her head. "I should do it. I think I can feel him, and he trusts me more than you."

"Very well." Another doubtful glance. He stepped back, although not very far, ready to jump in if necessary. Ally knelt down beside the creature. The blue man lay still, watching her intently, as she reached out and began to saw carefully at the tangled net.

The more strands she cut through, the more the net began to unravel. She could see an injury on the creature's thigh, then realised he was naked, and definitely male. Her eyes lingered on that blue flesh until she realised what she was doing, then went back to cutting. The net loosened beneath her fingers and the creature moved, as if testing his bonds.

She glanced over her shoulder to Aiden. "I think he can—" She never finished the words. The blue man sprang up, the remains of the net were thrown aside, and sand scattered everywhere as he sprinted toward the sea.

Aiden's hand gripped her shoulder to hold her steady as she stumbled back and fell onto the sand. "Are you all right?"

Ally nodded, but she was focused on the blue man. He had come to a stop at the edge of the water and now turned to stare back at her. For a moment they exchanged... something. Ally wasn't sure whether it was a mental image or a connection or a thank you. Then he turned and ran far enough into the water to allow him to dive. Although they watched the surface for some moments, he never reappeared.

Aiden offered his hand and Ally took it, letting him tug her to her feet. She brushed sand from her jeans, trying not to shiver. The air was colder than it had been and they needed to get moving again.

"So that was a storm kelpie," Aiden said thoughtfully.

"I thought they were just a story to frighten children."

"Like the Destroyer and the incubus," Aiden muttered. "But those were Stewart's creatures. Stewart's doing. Could this be another one?" He turned and looked around him. "Is Stewart here?"

"I don't know what you mean. You need to explain."

He turned to look at her and his dark eyes were so serious her smile died. "Stewart. The man... the thing we are trying to capture. He has con-trol of all manner of demons and creatures, to help him best us. First it was the Destroyer, then a demon known as an incubus that tried to take

Linny into the Underworld. Now this blue man."

Then, as if remembering there was danger everywhere, he strode toward Loki, calling to him. Alison sighed and followed, ignoring the ache in her legs. She had spent too much time knitting and not enough exercising, something she would have to rectify.

Then she watched in startled amazement as Aiden began to flicker on and off like a faulty lightbulb.

She had lived a strange life, but this had to be one of the strangest days in that life.

Chapter Fourteen

———

LOKI HAD RUN to the water's edge as soon as he was released, in search of more excitement. He let out a howl of frustration when he returned, unable to find any more blue men.

"You should be grateful you didn't get torn to pieces," Aiden said as he pat his dog. He still wasn't convinced that the blue man, or storm kelpie as Ally called him, was innocent. She might believe it was just a poor trapped creature desperate for help, but Aiden had seen enough of the otherworldly to doubt it was to be trusted.

It might very well be one of Stewart's creatures. Even now, Stewart might somehow be using it to bring about the downfall of the Hellfire Club. He was on his way to Moyle, Nicholas and Linny were on Moyle, Aiden was on Moyle, and all of that was too much of a coincidence. There was trouble ahead, and they needed to be ready for it.

He glanced back at Ally and felt a sensation in his chest, a squeeze of fear. When the blue man had darted up, he'd thought, just for a moment, that he was going to grab her and drag her into the ocean. That hadn't happened, but he still felt that fear. He trusted her, but nevertheless he wanted to take control, stand between her and anything that might be dangerous. He couldn't remember feeling like this before with anyone, let alone a woman who was still a stranger.

Well, there had been one long ago, but she hadn't been a stranger. And to his eternal shame, he had failed her miserably.

The women of the Hellfire Club had been too many to remember their faces, let alone their names. He had never felt more for them than a passing interest and they had been quickly forgotten whenever they left. It was amazing what enough bottles of claret could do to one's moral judgement.

He had, he admitted, been a selfish bastard then. An uncaring man. But the Sorceress had shown him why he had been like this, and though they were not excuses, they had let him understand himself better, and he had worked hard at becoming the new, improved version of Aiden Sutcliffe.

Since he'd returned to the mortal world, he hadn't had the opportunity to know many women other than the McNab sisters, who he thought of only as friends.

And he wasn't certain he wanted to find love the way that Lorne and Nicholas had. He had doubts that he was even capable of it. That he had these feelings for Ally MacDonald-Ellis now worried him, yes, but at the same time it allowed him to believe there might be a happy future for him out there somewhere. One day. But first, they needed to deal with Stewart.

Ally joined him, shading her eyes to stare out to the sea.

"So that was a storm kelpie," he said. He didn't mention that it was strange they had only been discussing the subject a short while ago, and now one had appeared. A coincidence? Perhaps. But he had grown suspicious of coincidences.

"You might think I'm insane, but I felt sorry for it. I felt a connection," she admitted. "I could feel its fear and pain. Who are we to judge something like that? They've been written about for centuries, but it stands to reason they have been with us for much longer than that. Yes, in the winter they are said to bring on the storms that cause ships to sink and sailors to drown, but in the summer they bask on the surface and sleep." Ally turned to him, her auburn hair blowing into her face. She caught it and held it back. "Some think that they were brought to these islands by the Norsemen as slaves. I think they're misunderstood, feared because we don't understand them. Strangers to our homeland have rarely been welcomed with open arms."

Slaves. Ice filled Aiden's heart at that word, and he feared it might show on his face. Loki came running back to them and he hid his feelings by bending to ruffle his dog's head. The dog flopped down and gazed at him lovingly.

"You have both been through a lot," Alison said.

Aiden cleared his throat, locking up the bad memories, just as he always did. "We have," he agreed. He remembered waking in the pet cemetery at Blackfriars Abbey. He now wondered if Loki had reassessed his past life, as Aiden had done, over the hundreds of years he had been asleep. Had the dog anything to be ashamed of? Somehow, he could not imagine Loki worrying too much about past transgressions. He was far more concerned about where his next meal was coming from or where his companions might be.

A gust of wind blew across the beach and Ally looked up at the sky with a frown. "More weather coming," she said.

"We'd better get to town then," said Aiden, and reached out his hand. It was instinctive, and before he could withdraw it, she'd slid her fingers into his.

They stood a moment with hands clasped, awkward, and then she let go and moved back toward the scooter. Aiden followed, trying not to look at her tight trousers beneath her coat. She was tall enough that he would not need to crick his neck if he tried to kiss her, or crush her if he tried to hold her. Indeed, superficially she was the perfect woman for him.

Was that why the Sorceress had chosen her for him? She had chosen Maggie for Lorne, and Aiden suspected the same was true of Linny and Nicholas. Was her plan to entangle him with Ally to the point where he was willing to do whatever he was told? He had thought the witch more subtle than that.

He knew by the way she had so enjoyed seeing Lorne and Nicholas falling in love that part of her must be a romantic. Perhaps it was now Aiden's turn to provide her with amusement?

He wasn't sure he was happy about his personal weaknesses and feelings being fodder for that frightening being.

Ally started the scooter. She settled on the seat and looked back at him, probably wondering why he was staring at her. Aiden hoped it hadn't been obvious he had been ogling her long legs and rounded bottom. He was getting hard and it would be rather embarrassing if she felt his cock nudging her as they drove. He pretended to give Loki another pat while he calmed his libido, then climbed on behind her, slipping his arms loose around her.

He needn't have worried that he was going to embarrass himself. The track was rough, and if the scooter wasn't bouncing over ruts and through potholes, it was swerving to avoid them. He could only hope to stay on, and whenever Ally's hair slapped into his face, he told himself the sting was good for him.

More cottages began to appear beside the track, and when they rounded a corner and came out of the shelter of a rounded hill, the town suddenly lay before them. It sprawled in the vicinity of a small bay with a jetty, and must once have been quaint and pretty, but times had changed it. A hotel now stood like a monolith in the midst of these charming cottages, all glass and metal, and Aiden stared at it in amazement.

The five-storey tower was not designed to blend in, but rather to stand out. Someone, Aiden thought, had had enough power to force it through what was perhaps an unwilling community. He couldn't imagine it had been a popular choice.

Ally seemed to be aware of his sudden silence.

"Makes a statement, doesn't it?" She said in a dry voice as she began to slow the scooter. "There was a lot of opposition, but the owner of the island wasn't going to let that stop him."

Aiden stared at the monstrosity. "The owner?" She had mentioned that before, someone owning the island, but he'd had other things on his mind.

"A rich American bought Moyle ten years ago. He loved the quaintness of the place, or so he said, but then he decided to build that."

Aiden's heart began to sink. American? Could it be Stewart? Why had they not heard of this before? Maggie and her deceased husband, Simon Frazer, had both been to the island in the last ten years. Simon's ancestors had lived here, and he had written a book about it. Maggie had visited the island with him, and she had scattered his ashes here when he died.

He felt a shiver pass over his skin, and despite the wind in his ears and the rumble of the scooter, there was a moment of stillness deep inside. Why had they not heard about this American owner before? He needed his friends. He needed to understand what was going on, and he couldn't do that on his own.

They were passing some of the cottages now. A goat bleated, causing Loki to let out a yelp and veer to the side. He didn't pursue this new curiosity, being wary after his encounter with the blue man.

Aiden heard the roar of an aeroplane overhead and looked up as a sleek silver body flew low over the island.

"Visitors will be coming in for the ceilidh," Alison explained with a smirk. "The well-heeled type. Rich," she added, for his benefit. Not that it was needed. He had picked up quite a bit of modern lingo since he had awoken.

"So this American isn't willing to live on Moyle in isolation?" he asked. "I would have thought that was part of its charm."

"No, he wants to make it into a rich man's paradise. The islanders are beginning to wonder what's next. More hotels? A resort above the beach that no one else can enjoy? Fancy shops and restaurants and everything that is anathema to small island living?"

Aiden noticed a lone protester standing with a sign a little way from the entrance to the hotel. The message, in untidy red paint, read "Give US Back OUR Island!"

"Is there nothing they can do to stop him?" Aiden asked, though he didn't mean the lone protester.

"He owns the island," she replied patiently, raising her eyebrows at him. "Unfortunately, that means he owns anyone who lives here, too. He can do what he likes. There were a number of meetings before the hotel was built but he didn't attend them. He sent his lackies and lawyers. I think we all knew then that there was nothing we could say to stop him. It was even suggested that if we weren't happy, there were daily ferries to the mainland and we should catch one."

She parked the scooter near a cairn that acted as a public bench. Aiden climbed off and glanced about as Loki trotted to his side. Apart from the protestor, the town seemed deserted. In the sheltered area near the jetty, a few boats rocked at anchor, while further out to sea, white horses were running atop the waves.

He realised Ally was eying him strangely. "What is it?"

"It's just… Well, you keep flickering on and off. I mean, you're visible for a moment and then you vanish again. It happened on the beach and now…"

His heart sank. "What about now?"

"Invisible," she said.

He wanted to swear but grit his teeth instead. "I hoped I was over that. What have I done wrong?"

Ally didn't bother trying to answer that. "Perhaps you should wait here with Loki while I ask about your friends? Then we can decide what to do. Perhaps they'll have some ideas."

Aiden caught hold of Loki by the scruff. "Very well. But hurry."

Ally gave a sympathetic nod before disappearing inside the hotel. He stared after her as the door slid shut. He could see a reflection of the street and the sky in the glass, the protestor a little way behind him, and Loki. A moment later, there Aiden was. His sudden appearance was startling enough for himself, but it was far worse for the protester with the placard. The man gave a wild cry, and bolted around the corner, abandoning his sign on the ground.

Chapter Fifteen

———————

BEHIND THE DESK, Mrs Shaw gave Ally a vacuous smile. "Can I help?" The fact that Ally knew Mrs Shaw and had dealt with her many times before didn't seem to make any difference to the woman.

There were some elements on the island who believed the hotel was a good thing, and when Ally had expressed an opposing opinion, she had been told that she shouldn't be interfering in island politics when she wasn't born and bred here. Mrs Shaw was one of those firmly on the side of turning Moyle into a playground for the rich and famous. All the same, this pretence that she and Mrs Shaw were strangers irritated the hell out of her, though Ally was damned if she was going to show it.

"I'm here to set up my pop-up shop," she said brightly. She waved toward the foyer. "Point me in the right direction."

Glazed eyes stared back at her.

"Or," Ally suggested with forced patience, "call the manager so he can do it."

"What a good idea." With exaggerated care and

a smile that was more like a smirk, Mrs Shaw reached for the phone.

Ally stopped her. "But before you do that, could you ring up to Mr Nicholas Darlington's room? I have his friend outside."

Squinty eyes now. "You mean the Earl of Northcote?"

"Do I? I only know him as Nicholas Darlington."

"Well, I have him down as the Earl of Northcote. He is staying in a suite with the Marquis of Lorne."

Alison wanted to laugh. Aiden hadn't told her that his friends were titled gentlemen. Not that it made much difference to her, being the daughter of one herself.

"Call one of them down, please. Their friend is waiting outside."

Mrs Shaw looked mulish. She was certainly going to refuse when her gaze went over Ally's head and her eyes widened. A deep voice spoke a moment later.

"I need to speak to the Earl of Northcote. Please tell him Lord Sutcliffe has arrived." Aiden was there, fully visible, with Loki at his side. Mrs Shaw's eyes focussed on the dog and she opened her mouth to protest, only to close it again when Aiden spoke in the sort of voice that was used to being obeyed. "Now, if you please."

Mrs Shaw took in Aiden's large, rugged form, and smiled in a sycophantic way before she scurried to do his bidding.

Ally leaned close to him and murmured,

"Clearly, you have more clout than me."

"I thought I should come in while everyone could still see me." He frowned. "She doesn't like you. Why?"

"She thinks I am stifling progress on the island. There is a clear line of demarcation on Moyle, Aiden. Those in favour of what the owner is doing and those who aren't."

"And you're one of the latter," he said, his lips twitching.

"Most definitely."

"The earl is on his way down," Mrs Shaw's announcement interrupted them. She shot Ally a cold stare. Ally asked herself what Mrs Shaw would have done if she'd reminded her that her brother had illegally distilled whiskey in the old days, and her mother had sold it from the front room of their cottage. But it didn't seem worth the effort.

Mrs Shaw began to click at something on her computer. "The manager?" Ally reminded her with a polite smile.

"I'll see if he's available," she said, and sauntered through a door behind the desk, closing it behind her.

Ally went across the foyer to the spot she was hoping to use for the pop-up shop. It was out of the way of general foot traffic, but still easily visible to anyone coming through the front door or using the lift. She could imagine a bored visitor gravitating toward her knitted wares, looking for something to take home and show off to their friends, or searching for something authentically Moyle.

Then, once they returned home, word would spread. People would start contacting her. Before they knew it, Ally and her ladies would be inundated with orders.

That was the hope, anyway.

Her friends had all worked very hard for this moment, and it was irritating that someone like Mrs Shaw was letting her personal spite get in her way. Ally was optimistic that even without this opportunity they could still make a success of the business, but the shop could fast track them into bigger markets.

Assuming there was still a world to sell to. Guilt rose up like a lump in her throat. She had been running from her past for so long and thought she'd escaped it, but now she feared she had brought it with her. Had she contaminated Moyle? But before she could go down that rabbit hole, she heard the doors to the elevator open. Loki gave one of his strange, almost human howls as two couples hurried over to Aiden.

She recognised Nicholas Darlington and Linny McNab from the cottage the other day. The other man was dark-haired and extremely good looking, and the woman accompanying him had curly dark hair. The group moved to welcome Sutcliffe and Loki with great smiles of relief.

"Aiden!" the curly-haired woman called out. This had to be Maggie. It wasn't until she threw her arms around the big man that Ally realised she was pregnant. Aiden hugged her back, his face full of joy and relief.

"Where were you?" The man who had to be the Marquis of Lorne gave Aiden a one-armed hug at the same time that Nicholas pounded him on the back.

Right at that moment, Aiden vanished, blinking out like someone had thrown a light switch. There was a shocked silence. Ally tried not to laugh at the looks of shock on their faces.

Maggie gasped. "Where'd he go?"

"He's still here," Lorne said, tightening his grip. "I'm still holding him."

"Ow! I know I'm still here," Aiden growled. "I've been invisible, but I thought I was over it. Bloody hell!" He made it sound like he'd had a cold.

"But why were you invisible?" Linny asked. "What is the point of that? Is it the witchy woman's idea? God, is anything too low for her?"

"That is so unfair." Maggie waved a hand in front of her face. "Sorry, getting a bit emotional here!"

Lorne slid an arm around her waist and kissed her cheek.

"Don't move," Nicholas instructed Aiden. "We don't want to lose you."

"It's not as if I can't see you, you know. Ally!" Aiden sounded frantic, and Ally moved over to him.

"It's all right." She tried to sound calm and in control. "Take my hand, please. That worked before; perhaps it will again."

The others stood back as Ally's hand fumbled

its way down Aiden's chest. His hand took hers and squeezed so hard she felt her bones creak. A heartbeat later, he blinked on again. Was it a coincidence? She supposed it might be, but she didn't think so, and she was prepared to keep holding his hand just in case.

His dark eyes had become a little glazed as they stared into hers. He stood very close, and he put his arm around her shoulders while his other hand clutched her hand as if he wasn't going to ever let it go.

"I thought I was better," he said miserably.

"It's all right. You're back." Ally found herself patting his lower back, and it was only when she looked up and found the others staring at her that she stopped. Aiden's friends' faces showed emotions ranging from amusement to polite interest to rampant speculation.

"We were at your friend's cottage earlier," Nicholas said to Aiden. "Were you there then? Why didn't you say something, Sutcliffe?"

"I tried! I couldn't make myself seen or heard then. It was hellishly frustrating. When I tried to grab you, my hands went right through. It's a wonder you couldn't feel me."

Nicholas shuddered at the image this evoked.

"Loki knew," Linny pointed out. "He was desperate to get back to you after we took him with us. That's why he broke his lead, wasn't it? He was trying to tell us you were there, but we didn't understand."

Hearing his name, Loki yawned and trotted around the group. Linny gave him a good scratch, telling him what a good boy he was, before wrinkling her nose.

"Phew, he smells like rotting seaweed."

"We were down on the beach," Ally said.

Aiden added in a serious voice, "We saw something on the way here."

Lorne's face turned hard. "Stewart?" He tightened his arm around Maggie.

"No. I don't know if it had anything to do with him, but it might." Aiden went on to explain their encounter with the storm kelpie.

Nicholas agreed with Aiden's assessment. "We can't be sure it wasn't one of Stewart's creatures." The frown he gave made his scar more prominent.

Aiden nodded. "Ally said she hasn't seen anything like this here on Moyle before. It seems odd that it has suddenly appeared now."

Ally jumped in. "As far as I know, one hasn't been seen in a very long time. In living memory, in fact."

"We should assume that Stewart is playing his games," Lorne said.

"Is he here yet?" Aiden asked abruptly. "Have you seen him?"

"No. We think he's going to be here for the ceilidh. Perfect opportunity for him to start playing his games," Nicholas said.

"Oh!" Linny looked up in surprise. "You've gone again, Aiden. Now he's back."

Aiden groaned and clutched Ally's hand as if it were a lifeline. So far, their little group had kept his 'problem' from prying eyes, although the hotel lobby was empty apart from Mrs Shaw. But now a tall, thin man strolled toward them. "Miss MacDonald-Ellis?"

Ally tried to clear her mind of the distracting heat and feel of Aiden so close to her and focused her attention on the man. "Yes?"

"Mrs Shaw said you were inquiring about space for your shop for this weekend?"

"Ah, I wasn't so much asking as wondering where you wanted it. I already have permission to set up."

He frowned. "Not from me. We have made plans for a whiskey theme."

Ally stared at him, for a moment speechless. Her voice turned husky with anger. "We've been working on this for months. I was told that we could have the shop in the foyer and we've been—"

"Not by me," he repeated. "I only came into this job a fortnight ago, and we are planning a whiskey theme. We now have several distilleries on board. There is no room for knitware." He made the word sound as if she were asking to set up a stand of cheap socks.

She took a breath, not sure whether she was going to shout at him or... she was probably going to shout at him.

"Miss MacDonald-Ellis has put a lot of work into this," Aiden said firmly. He moved so that she became sandwiched between him and the manager, who took a smart step back. "I for one would find an exhibit of local craftwork and cul ture more agreeable than nothing but whiskey displays."

Ally put a hand on his chest to stop him and cleared her throat. "The manager... the previous manager was a friend of one of the women in my knitting group. He promised we could have a spot in the foyer."

Linny eyed her curiously. "Did you sign anything?"

"No. It was a verbal agreement. That is the way we do things here on Moyle." With a glare at the man, whose frown had darkened.

Linny now stepped in. "Lord Sutcliffe is right. Not everyone is interested in whiskey, although in my experience, too much of it can certainly make you spend up big. Clever thinking," with a wink at the manager. "But there will be non-whiskey drinkers here at the ceilidh—and I am not stereotyping by saying 'women'—who would be thrilled to see a stall of Moyle knitting. You may not realise this, but authentic artisan clothing is considered high fashion at the moment. I am very disappointed you aren't supporting the locals." She clasped Nicholas's arm. "The Earl of Northcote here is particularly interested in knitware."

Ally bit her lip to stop a smile as Nicholas tried to smooth the look of panic on his face.

"I am indeed a great fan of the knitted sweater," he agreed.

"As are we all," Aiden added firmly.

Ally launched into the fray again. "Visitors will have a number of colours and motifs to choose from," she said. "They can take their pick, and if we don't have what they want on hand, then we can make it and deliver it to them. We're shipping worldwide."

There was a heavy silence. The manager looked from one to the other of them and then swallowed. "Well, of course, if the earl wishes there to be knitted wares, I can always bring some in from the mainland. I believe there is a factory in Edinburgh that—"

"Moyle knitting," Maggie broke in, eyes flashing. "It is unique. A mixture of Shetland, Hebridean, and Scandinavian. The Marquis was thinking of selling a selection from Blackfriars Abbey once it is reopened to the public. Isn't that so, Lorne?"

There was a sparkle in his ice blue eyes. "Very true, my love."

The manager was on the back foot now. He looked around, slightly frantic, as if hoping for rescue, but his staff, even Mrs Shaw, were conspicuously absent. He gave in with bad grace.

"Very well," he said. "I will see what I can do. Miss MacDonald-Ellis, follow me."

Ally trotted obediently after him.

"This time, get it in writing," Linny hissed.

Ally gave a thumbs up without turning.

Chapter Sixteen

———◆———

NOW THAT THEY no longer had manag-
ers or receptionists to deal with, Maggie
squeezed Aiden's arm affectionately. "So good to
see you, Aiden. We missed you."

He felt his cheeks ache from his broad smile and
moisture gathered in his eyes. If he wasn't careful,
he'd start to sob. "And I you. All of you. After the
bomb went off in Port Finlay… I thought you
might be dead. Properly dead."

He looked about at his friends. There was so
much to discuss, and he needed to ask them what
plans they had devised so far. But not here.

Nicholas put a firm hand on his shoulder.
"Come," he said, as if reading his mind. "We need
to talk somewhere more private."

Back in the suite, Aiden flickered off and on a
number of times, both to their amusement and
concern. Lorne and Nicholas gave a brief sum-
mary of what had happened to them since Port
Finlay, and how they had ended up on Moyle—
which was still rather a mystery, as far as Aiden
could tell. Then he shared his own account.

"The Sorceress seems to want Ally to be with

us at the end, when we capture Stewart." At least, that was what Aiden had understood of their conversation. He didn't think it necessary to add that the Sorceress also seemed to be playing matchmaker again, and that he was coming around to the idea.

"So for one reason or another, we're all here on Moyle," Lorne said with a humourless smile. "Is that Stewart's doing or the Sorceress?"

Aiden remembered something. He turned to Maggie, who was tucked up into the corner of the sofa, half asleep. "Ally told me that this island was bought by an American ten years ago. This hotel was built by him. Half the islanders didn't want it, but he went ahead with it anyway."

Maggie blinked and sat up at that. "Shortly before he died, Simon said someone had bought Moyle. He often dreamed about buying it himself, or at least helping some of the islanders purchase it jointly. But then he was ill and…" She heaved a sigh. "When I was here with his ashes, I wasn't all that concerned about local politics." Then, making the connection, she shrugged off the past, her eyes widening. "An American? You don't think…?"

The group exchanged speculative glances.

"It has to be Stewart," Maggie decided. "Either directly or indirectly. He's always several steps ahead of us. He took over Simon's form and pretended to be him. This is the next move in his game, isn't it? To sully the island Simon loved. Moyle is now his and he can do what he wants with it. He'll make it his little kingdom, and he's brought us here to marvel at his cleverness before he thrusts the dagger into our hearts. Metaphorically, of course."

"Not if we have anything to say about it," Lorne replied. "Metaphorically or otherwise." Nicholas and Aiden nodded in agreement.

The conversation died and everyone took a moment to relax and collect their thoughts, giving Aiden a chance to observe how things had changed among the others. Lorne and Maggie seemed even closer than he remembered, the little touches between them, the glances of deep understanding. And though he hadn't seen how close Nicholas and Linny were at the cottage earlier, he could now tell that their relationship had undergone a change.

Nicholas had been mooning over Linny ever since they met at Blackfriars Abbey, but until now Linny had never reciprocated. Now Linny cuddled up to Nicholas's side, comfortable in his presence, and much more than that. It was love, pure and simple.

Aiden felt more alone than he had in quite some time. His friends would always be part of his life, but his world was changing. Whatever happened here over the next few days, he doubted things would be the same ever again. They may triumph, they may capture Stewart, they may even be allowed to stay in this century and live their lives, but change was still inevitable.

He was surprised he wasn't made more miserable by that conclusion. Was it because of Ally? She had brought hope, warmth and humour into his life, as well as a growing desire.

Loki lay sprawled at his feet and, as if he had heard his master's thoughts, the animal raised his head, alert.

Then a knock sounded on the door.

———◆———

Ally knocked on the door. She heard voices inside. Her business with the manager had taken longer than she'd expected. He hadn't been happy, but he had listened to her ideas, and reluctantly agreed to what she asked. He even admitted there were some items she had ordered weeks ago waiting in the storage cupboard, and he would get them out. All the while, Mrs Shaw glared at her from over his shoulder as she took notes.

Once she was alone, Ally rang Mrs Morison and explained the situation. Most of the garments were already at the cottage of Mrs MacKenzie, who lived closer to the hotel, but a few of the showcase items were still at Ally's cottage. She and Mrs Morison agreed that she would need help getting them all to the hotel.

"My nephew Hamish will help. He's a good lad," Mrs Morison had said. "He can gather everything up and bring it over. We can set up today and be ready for the ceilidh tomorrow night. There are certain to be guests looking for something to do."

"Thank you, that sounds perfect. Oh, and there's Wayward. Can he feed her? It's just that I don't know when I'll get home. There's so much to do."

And a two hundred-year-old man who needs my help, but she didn't add that.

"Of course he can, Ally. No trouble."

Ally sighed with relief. It was good to have friends. She had just finished the phone call when Mrs Shaw entered the room.

"The Marquis and his guests request your presence in their suite," she said grandly, as if it was a royal summons.

So here she was.

Linny opened the door and smiled at her. Now that she had kicked off her high heels, she was a lot shorter than Ally.

"All good?" she asked.

"Yes, they were happy to give me what I wanted," Ally said. "Well, happy might not be the right word, but I got what I wanted. Thanks."

"No bother," Linny said with a wave of her hand. "Come in. We are having a bit of a war council."

The suite was more luxurious than anything Ally had ever seen on Moyle. She followed Linny to a massive sofa and deep armchairs, which were occupied by the others. Loki yawned and got to his feet, padding over to her for a pat and then escorting her the rest of the way.

The three men leaned toward each other intently, deep in conversation. Maggie was dozing in the corner of the sofa, tucked up in a colourful blanket.

"Boys, Ally's here," Linny called out.

Aiden, who'd had his back to her, jumped up. "Ah, there you are. Come in. Sit down." His friends exchanged amused glances over his eagerness.

"It's all right," she said. "I didn't mean to interrupt."

"Did you get what you wanted from the manager?" Lorne asked in a droll voice. "I hope we terrified him sufficiently."

Ally smiled. "It was fine. Everything's fine. I've asked for one of my friends to bring in the rest of the merchandise so that I don't have to go home." She paused, wondering if that sounded presumptuous, then added, "Well, not just that. Mrs Morison's nephew will be feeding Wayward too." Was she gabbling? Maybe. She wasn't normally so nervous.

"Wayward?" Nicholas asked.

"Cat," Aiden explained. "Or demon, I'm not certain which."

Linny settled down on the sofa beside Nicholas and cuddled in. "How did Loki cope with that?"

"He was fine. Wayward is probably scarred for life," Ally responded, deadpan.

They laughed. Maggie gave a start and a little snort and opened her eyes. She saw everyone staring at her and sighed. "God, sorry. I can't seem to help it."

"Don't apologise," said Linny. "You're sleeping for two. Your little Marquis needs his rest."

Maggie flushed, hand on her belly. "Not so little. His empire grows every day."

Lorne lifted her feet onto his lap and began to rub them with loving thoroughness.

Aiden cleared his throat. "We were talking

about the American who now owns the island," he said. "No one seems to know anything about him, which is suspicious in itself. Do you know his name?" He looked at Ally.

"I think it was Frazer. There was some talk he had ancestors here and wanted to return to his roots. To be honest, I was too frustrated to take much notice."

Maggie stiffened. "It's Stewart," she whispered.

Aiden turned to Ally. "Maggie was married to Professor Frazer. She's familiar with Moyle."

Ally nodded. She had heard something about the Professor, and had even read his book, but the fact that Maggie had been married to him had escaped her.

"Stewart likes to impersonate Simon," Maggie said bitterly. Her face looked drawn and tired, her eyes sad. "It amuses him."

"I think it is safe to assume the owner is Stewart," Lorne said.

Despite their willingness to include her, Ally was still an outsider. It was clear they had gone through much together, and it had created a bond between them. But she was happy for their help. Thanks to their intervention, her pop-up shop was back in business. That had been a huge relief. She didn't think she was going to tell the other women about the almost cancellation. They had enough to worry about. As far as they knew, everything was proceeding as planned.

Suddenly Aiden blinked off, but this time he came back again almost at once, which seemed like progress. She found her gaze lingering on him. She told herself it was to see if he disappeared again and needed to make contact with her to reappear. But his handsome face and his square jaw, those broad shoulders and tall, muscled body were reason enough.

Alison had steered clear of emotional attachments after her first boyfriend, who'd ran a mile after she'd had a late night encounter with a desperate spirit. She had doubted any man would understand her life, and now she'd found one who understood all too well. But he came with more than a little baggage of his own.

She had always understood what those boys she had dated would have felt like when confronted with her issues, which was why she had kept it to herself. But now it was her turn. Did she really want to add Aiden Sutcliffe to her already complicated life? Was he worth the trouble that was bound to follow? To her surprise, she rather thought he was.

She had to admit, they were an interesting group. She tried to imagine the three men out of their jeans and sweaters, instead dressed in the attire of gentlemen from the early 1800s. Lorne was a dark angel, while Nicholas Darlington had the look of a gentleman pirate. They seemed familiar with one another in a way normally reserved for brothers, but then they had been through an awful lot. And, according to Aiden, there was still more to come before they could even think of relaxing and living their lives. Everything was up in the air until Stewart was captured and his plans foiled. Everything hinged on that.

As for their partners, Maggie seemed to be the serious one, listening closely to the others before putting her own point across. With her wild, dark hair and intense gaze, Alison could picture her as a woman with a mission she was determined to fulfill. The way Lorne put his arm about her and kissed her cheek was also rather cute, but Ally wondered about the future of their child.

Linny, with her straight fair hair and smart mouth, already knew how to make her laugh. Yet she was gentle with Nicholas, despite her teasing, and he seemed very protective, as if he would take on the world for her. Passion simmered between them.

So where did Ally fit in? Was she just passing through their story, a brief footnote, or was her future linked to theirs by the mysterious Stewart?

As if hearing her thoughts, Aiden glanced up at her. Something flared in his gaze, an emotion that was there and gone before she could recognise it. A smile tugged at his firm lips. She smiled back. She couldn't help it, and all manner of emotions rose up inside her. Want and desire, need and understanding.

"We have to search the island," Maggie said. "We can't wait for Stewart to come to us."

"But will searching do any good?" Nicholas asked. "If he doesn't want to be found, then he won't be. You know that, Maggie. We can spend days looking and he'll be laughing at us, waiting to get us at our weakest moment."

"Then what do you suggest?"

Ally spoke up. "The ceilidh." They turned to

her in surprise. She knew she was right. "He'll be there. If he's the sort of man Aiden said he was, then he'll want a grand entrance and an even grander climax. He's not so subtle that he won't want to take the stage, is he?"

"No, he's not that subtle," Aiden agreed. "In fact, I would say he lives for the stage."

"He'll want to take us out with a bang." This came from Nicholas. "And he'll probably have plenty of helpers along with him. As well as creatures both from this world and the other. He knows their weaknesses, and he'll use that to get them to dance to his tune."

Their eyes were now fixed on her.

"Aiden told us about your ability to talk to the dead," Lorne said. "It seems awfully strange that we are here on Moyle, too. Do you think perhaps your fate is linked to ours?"

She bit her lip for a moment before lifting her head. "I don't know," she admitted reluctantly, "but it has crossed my mind."

"The guru," Aiden said swiftly. Then, explaining to the others, "Alison's father had a guru in his cult when she was young. He was very focussed on her abilities."

"And you think it could have been Stewart, playing the long game?" Linny asked with a sceptical lift of her brows.

"There is more to it than that," Aiden looked to Ally. "Tell them the rest," he said.

"This man said I was 'the one,' and spoke about the end of days. I assumed at first that he meant I could prevent the end of the world, but then I learned he meant I would cause it." She suddenly felt queasy. She didn't want that responsibility. It was one of the reasons she had ended up here in Moyle.

Maggie leaned forward. "What was he like, this guru?"

"He was Armenian, dark-skinned, very charismatic. He had everyone, including my father, in the palm of his hand."

The three men exchanged a meaningful glance.

"It's possible." Lorne turned to the others, he explained. "When we brought the Destroyer into the world, it was with the help of an Egyptian. At least, that was what he called himself. That man was Stewart's mentor, and his abuser. I think Stewart would enjoy stealing his identity, but perhaps we are giving him too much credit."

"All the same," Aiden mused, "we need to consider the possibility. Stewart has been planning his big finale for a very long time. We know he can be extremely patient. He's worked on some of his vicious little plans for centuries."

"He hates you." Maggie was paler than before, as she reached to clasp Lorne's hand.

Aiden agreed. "It's you he will focus on. He will want you here, front and centre, when he lifts the curtain on his final act. We have to remember that, Lorne. We can use it against him."

Lorne looked at his friend, as if surprised he was taking a leading role, and then nodded.

"You're right, Aiden," he said. "Happy to be used."

Chapter Seventeen

———

THEY ORDERED LUNCH, and as the afternoon drew on, Maggie slipped away for a nap, followed by Lorne, and soon after that Nicholas and Linny left for their own room. After a great deal of whining and sad looks, a bed was made out of some sofa rugs and a cushion for Loki, and the dog settled down with a happy groan.

Ally chuckled and Aiden rolled his eyes. It was good to find something to smile at because she was worried. Now that she knew what the others had been through, she understood how dangerous this Stewart person was. He was a chameleon, able to take on new identities at will.

It seemed likely he was the guru from her teenage years, which made her a pawn in whatever game he was currently playing. Stewart was a man on a mission, and his scheme had been unfolding for a very long time. But it seemed the endgame was finally upon them. They needed to find a way to stop this dangerous man with the least amount of damage.

Aiden reached out and stroked a finger lightly

between her brows. She felt the warmth of his rough fingertip against her skin.

"You're frowning," he said. "What are you thinking about?"

"I can't help wondering if all this was meant to be. That I was always destined to be here, to meet you and the others. Maybe that's why I was drawn to Moyle in the first place. And whatever is about to happen will involve me as well as the Hellfire Club."

Aiden shifted uncomfortably. "I don't like the word 'destined'," he said. "It implies that everything Stewart wishes to do is pre-ordained, or that we lack free will in our actions. I believe we can stop it. We can defeat Stewart. We have before. We just have to puzzle out how to do it, and you are here to help us with that."

She nodded, feeling a rush of confidence. "So I'm here to help you put an end to Stewart's insanity? I like that. Better than bringing about the end of times."

"To be frank, I think he's overreached himself."

"You think he's juggling too many balls. That he's bound to drop one."

Aiden nodded in agreement.

Ally leaned back against the cushions and closed her eyes. She was tired. It had been a very strange few days, and it seemed there was still more to come. Her mind was full of questions and tasks that needed to be done, but her body needed time to re-energize. Just five minutes and she'd be ready to…

Aiden smiled as Ally slipped into slumber. Any-one who could fall asleep so easily must have a very clear conscience. Perhaps that was why it had never been easy for him. He leaned back, resisting the urge to stroke a finger down her face or tuck a strand of her auburn hair behind her ear.

This impulse was new to him and he knew he should feel strange about it, but he didn't. He and Ally had grown close in a short amount of time, had become the sort of team the Sorceress had wanted. Whether it would last or not he didn't know, but right now it was all he craved. These moments felt fragile and precious and he wanted to hang onto them.

He closed his eyes and allowed the soft sound of Ally's breathing to wash over him. Despite every-thing that was happening, he felt relaxed, even hopeful. Aiden wondered if that was because Ally was with him.

A moment later, he was asleep, hurtling into his own past. He heard the witch inside his head and realised too late that he had let down his guard and inadvertently let her slip behind the locked door inside his heart. It was too late now; he couldn't push her out. He could only allow some of the worst moments of his life to unfold before him.

He was a child, standing outside his father's dressing room, heart pounding, wanting to scream. He already knew what the Sorceress was doing. She was forcing him to relive a moment in his life that he had locked away, hoping to never think of again.

Too painful. Too shameful.

He saw his hand reach out and tried to stop it, but it was as if his eight-year-old body was acting in the way it had back then, even while his mind belonged to the grown man he was now. Like one of the movies he watched on television.

His small hand closed around the door latch and began to turn. He heard it now, the sounds that had drawn him here in the first place. Grunts and soft cries. A moan.

The door inched open.

Knowing what he was about to see made no difference. A lump of stone filled his chest.

'Don't,' he wanted to shout to the child Aiden. 'Stop.'

But of course, the man couldn't change any of this. They were but echoes of the past. A moment later, he was looking into the dressing room.

His father was on top of Essie, his naked buttocks pushing between her soft thighs. His face was red with effort, his hands clenched in her dark hair as they lay on the red velvet sofa.

Aiden's eyes widened. All he could think was that his father was hurting Essie, his beloved Essie. She may be only a servant, but she was the only person in this house who seemed to love him the way a parent should.

Perhaps he'd made a sound. His father looked up, his expression shocked at first, then furious. Not shame, just rage at being interrupted in his pleasure. Then Essie had twisted her head to see him too.

"No, Aiden," she whispered. "It is all right. Go now. Go."

He turned and fled, running out into the corridor.

He heard his mother's voice in her own room, as she ordered the maid to dress her, as if there was nothing happening in the other room. That her husband was not doing things to Essie.

Essie found him later that evening.

He knew she was there, but didn't look up from his book; his eyes focussed on the well-thumbed pages without seeing anything. After a moment, her soft steps moved closer, and he could smell the scent of her soap.

"Aiden, I am so sorry that you had to see. Your father…"

She brushed back his dark hair, but he pulled away. He didn't want her to touch him. He felt sick at the thought of what he had seen, full of hurt and betrayal and confusion.

"I will go, if that is what you wish," she said. "If you do not want to see me again, then I will go home. You will never see me again."

"Yes!" he shouted. "Go away! I never want to see you again."

She gave a soft sigh and left him to his rage and pain.

By the time he realised what he had done, when he went to look for her, to change her mind, she was gone.

It was later that he learned of his father's plantation in Grenada, of the men and women who slaved for him and made the Sutcliffe family wealthy. Of Essie, the woman he had brought home with him and used, and the wife who looked the other way because of the money that bought her pretty dresses and paid for her social engagements.

When he was old enough to accompany his father, he thought he knew everything. Yet the reality had been so much more than he had expected. He saw the casual cruelty and violence at play, and was sickened by the way the work-force was treated and shamed. He saw the hatred in their eyes when they thought their masters did not see.

He'd looked desperately for Essie, for he had never forgotten her. As he had grown older, he had realised she was the only one who had loved him unconditionally, and he had sent her away. He wished to make amends. He searched the island, asked questions, risked the scorn of the other masters and the slaves, but he never found her.

She was gone, and not knowing what had happened to her, how she had died, how she must have suffered… he could not sleep for a long time.

Nor could he forgive himself. The pain was always there, reminding him to never again feel so deeply. The knowledge that he would be hurt and he would hurt others. Never again would he delve into a situation, or take a side, in case it was the wrong one.

It was both the breaking and the making of Aiden Sutcliffe. The reason he had become the person he once was, until the Sorceress had sent him to sleep. And now she had made him relive it.

Chapter Eighteen

———◆———

ALLY WOKE TO the sound of a telephone. It was answered by someone—Aiden, his voice a low murmur. A moment later, he had come to her and she saw the worry in his eyes. She struggled to sit up. Someone had covered her with a blanket and placed a cushion under her head.

"That was Mrs Morison. She says she hasn't seen her nephew. He was supposed to come and pick her up so they could bring everything over here for the store, but he hasn't arrived. And he hasn't come here either. She said she rang the reception desk, but no one had seen him."

A stab of concern pierced Ally's sleepiness, and she was now wide awake. "That isn't like Hamish. He's very reliable."

The garments for the shop needed to be set up by tomorrow night at the latest. Aiden's friends might be making plans to take down a demon, but Ally still needed to worry about the future of the women on the island. And that meant making sure their business venture was successful. They had given her their trust and their acceptance, and she owed it to them not to go missing at this critical time.

She pushed her hair out of her eyes, aware of Aiden standing close, arms folded.

"What do you want to do?" he asked, his voice deep and soft. Ally tried to ignore the tingle of desire that voice instilled in her. Concentrate, she told herself. This is important.

"I'm trying to understand what happened. It's not like he could get lost on Moyle." Her mobile phone rang, which made her jump. She fumbled for it in her pocket and peered down at the number on screen. "It's Hamish," she said, relieved, and took the call.

But when she spoke his name, there was only silence on the other end, except for the sound of breathing. Goosebumps peppered her skin. Something in her expression made Aiden frown. He crouched down next to her, a warm hand resting on her knee.

"What is it?" he asked.

"I don't know." Then she spoke again into the phone. "Hamish? Where are you? Your aunt is worried."

"I'm at the boglach." He said in a rush, and there was something in the background, another voice, but too low for her to make out. "No." That was more of a groan than a word. He wasn't speaking to her, and her heart began to beat faster as she focussed on the boy on the other end of the line.

"Hamish," she said sharply. "Talk to me. What happened?"

A gasping breath and then, "Please…" before

the call cut off.

Ally stared at the phone a long moment, then looked up at Aiden.

"I heard some of that," he said.

"Hamish was… I've never heard him like that. He's always so cheerful and easy-going. He sounded as if he was terrified, and I can't imagine Hamish terrified."

"Where is he?" Aiden asked. "What's a boglach?"

"That's Gaelic for swamp or wetland, but it isn't that large, really. It's on the west of the island. And that's the other thing. Why would he be there? It's way out of his way." She stood up, tossing aside the colourful blanket. "It makes no sense, Aiden."

Aiden's face turned grim. "If you factor in Stewart, it makes perfect sense."

She felt numb. "Why would he do something to Hamish?"

"To get at you. Us. If it is Stewart, then he will have a reason."

"If what is Stewart?" Linny had come in unheard and now looked at them suspiciously, arms folded.

By the time Ally explained, the others had arrived, and had to be told as well. None of them were happy, and all suspected Stewart was involved. It fit his pattern.

"You can't go," Lorne said, as if his word was law. "It's a trap."

"I have to," Ally said, annoyed at his presumption. "I asked him to do me a favour, and I'm not going to leave him in the lurch. He might be hurt." Then, softly, "Stewart may have hurt him."

"She's right, Lorne. She can't leave him." Linny wasn't afraid to give Lorne a glare. "She has to go."

"But not alone," Aiden said. "I'm going with her,"

"Then I'm coming too," said Lorne.

"No!" everyone but Ally cried out.

"Lorne, you're the last person who should show up at any potential trap," said Darlington. "Not until we're ready for Stewart's endgame."

"I'll go then." This time it was Maggie volunteering, and the opposition was just as loud.

"No, Maggie," Lorne said when the noise had died down. "You're not going anywhere."

"And who are you to order me about?" Maggie responded.

"The man who loves you more than life," Lorne said, staring into her eyes. "The father of your unborn child who does not want it put at risk."

Maggie sighed, and her dark eyes glistened with tears.

"If Stewart wished to find a way to separate us, this could be it." Nicholas rubbed a thumb over his scar as he considered this. "Get some of us out of the hotel, leaving the others vulnerable. We can't let him do that. Lorne, you definitely can't go, and neither can Maggie."

"I'm not leaving my sister," Linny said in a way that brooked no arguments.

"And I'm not leaving you," Nicholas countered. They stared at each other, and then Linny smiled and glanced away.

"Fine. Whatever," she murmured.

"There is no need for debate," Aiden spoke with firm confidence. "I will go with Ally. I am expendable. The rest of you are not."

There was a shocked silence and then the objections started again, all of them crowding in. He shouldn't have used the word "expendable," but it was accurate. He raised his hand to stop them, stepping back.

"Ally and I will find Hamish," he repeated. "He needs our help. Ally is the only one who knows where to look, and I am best suited to keep her safe. We'll be careful."

There were more protests, but in the end, they accepted there was no other choice.

"Okay, but Loki should stay here." Linny wrapped her arms around the big dog. "I'm not sure running about loose on the island is a good idea for him. He might get you side-tracked, and you've had enough adventures recently, haven't you, boy?"

Loki appeared to agree.

———◆———

Aiden wasn't sure he would ever enjoy riding on the back of a scooter, but he was getting better at it. They started off slowly, leaving the town via a narrow rocky road that led inland. They climbed some hills, then wound their way down again. Aiden was entranced by the views around them.

The wind buffeted them on the exposed areas of the track. Clouds scudded across the grey sky, and in the distance, he could see rain falling over the sea. It was a wild place, very unfamiliar to him.

Grenada had been beautiful in its way as well, steamy and hot, the lush vegetation and the strange insects and animals. He had caught a fever while there and lain delirious in his bed for days, dreaming that Essie had come back to forgive him. She hadn't. She was gone and the opportunity for him to make amends had gone with her.

A strand of Ally's hair whipped his cheek, bringing him back to the present, and he buried his face into her shoulder. There was comfort in her scent and her warmth, and he was prepared to take full advantage of it... until he felt her start.

"Your hair," he explained.

"Oh, sorry, I should have tied it up."

"It's all right." And it was. The softness of her skin, the warmth of her body against his, the scent of her hair. Everything was all right to him. With her in his arms, he felt better than he had since... since before he turned eight.

Though he had been blinking in and out of sight occasionally, he felt fine. Ally made him feel stable in more ways than one. There was nothing that would have stopped him from coming with her to find Hamish. If Stewart tried to harm her, Aiden would fight him to the death. Not that he'd said that to Ally. He wasn't sure she would appreciate his chivalry. He'd learned from Linny and Maggie that in this modern world, women could fight their own battles and were insulted if you insinuated they could not.

Ally slowed down as they reached the top of another steeper hill, and they now cautiously descended the other side. It was getting more rocky and rugged, although as far as Aiden could see, there were no actual mountains on Moyle. He looked out to the west and saw nothing but ocean, the waves topped with white, the clouds making a pattern of colours on the water from darkest green to pale grey. It was breathtaking.

"I wonder how your storm kelpie friend is," he said in her ear.

She turned her head. "Why?"

"Just wondering. Doesn't look like the sort of weather for basking."

She laughed at that.

There were a couple of sheep in the middle of the track, and she manoeuvred around them, as they clearly had no intention of moving. Aiden couldn't help but chuckle as the sheep seemed to roll their eyes at him. One of them was chewing on a piece of greenery.

"These are Moyle sheep and mostly they roam free," Ally said. "We use their wool to make our knitwear."

"They look suitably impressed."

He felt her laugh against his chest. He supposed he should think it strange they were able to laugh in such circumstances, but it felt good. They felt good together.

There was another bend ahead and Ally was turning into it when there was a bang like a thunderclap. Startled, the scooter wobbled, and

Aiden looked up at the sky.

He didn't see any thunder clouds, but who knew what sort of weather Moyle was capable of? A moment later, Ally cried out, and he looked to where she was pointing.

In front of them lay a stretch of ground that could have been half a mile in diameter. It was pale green with the appearance of moss, and he could see patches of still water lying greasy upon the surface. The boglach. Dead trees rose in several parts of the swamp, their branches like rotting spars pointing to the grey sky. A large bird, that could have been an eagle perched on one of the branches, flapped away.

Aiden didn't have time to watch it go because his eyes were rivetted on the figure standing in the middle of the boglach. He was dressed in one of the Moyle patterned sweaters, and his back was to them, his arms stiff by his sides, holding himself very still.

"That's Hamish," Ally said. "What is he doing? It's not safe in there. The islanders say if you step on a shaky patch, it's bottomless."

Carefully she took the scooter up to the edge of the mossy area and stopped. Aiden stepped off while Ally pushed down the stand and joined him by the marsh. They stood, staring out over the shimmering mass of green weed and water. Aiden could see now that what he had thought was firm ground wasn't firm at all. How Hamish had got himself to the middle was anyone's guess.

"Hamish!" Ally called out.

Hamish jumped at the sound of her voice, and

wavered slightly. He tried to turn his head to see her, but immediately turned it back, his body stiffer than before. "I can't move," he shouted, his voice high and desperate. "He put me here, Ally, and I can't move."

"Who put you there?" She was already making her way around the edges of the boglach, circling it so that she could get in front of him.

"Mr Stewart. He said he was a friend of yours. He said he was going to help me bring your knitted things to the hotel, but then something happened and I...I don't know," he wailed. "Everything just went black. When I woke up, I was here, in the middle of the bog. I can't move, Ally. I'm afraid to try in case I start to sink." His voice broke. He was plainly terrified.

Ally quickened her steps and Aiden followed behind her. At one point, his foot sank into the soft ground, and then kept sinking until he was up to his knee in the foul stuff. He dragged himself free, feeling the suck of the boglach as if it was unwilling to let him go. It clung to his jeans and boot, and he wiped it off as best he could on the grass. Any foolish ideas he might have had of running across the surface to save the boy were dashed.

"Hamish, just stay still," Ally shouted. She hadn't seen what happened behind her and Aiden kept quiet. They had travelled far enough around the circumference of the marsh so that they were now in front of the boy, and Aiden could see his face was so white his freckles stood out like ink spots, his red hair standing up as if he'd been trying to tear it out in his despair. He was shivering, staring back at them with wide, frightened blue eyes.

"I can't get out," he whimpered. "You need to find Macaulay. He knows the way across. He'll save me, Ally."

"The boglach changes all the time," Ally reminded him. "No one can know for sure the way across."

"He can get me out," Hamish insisted. "Please, find him!"

"What if you lie flat? I've seen that done when Mr McIver rescued his dog."

"I'm afraid to," Hamish admitted. "Mr Stewart said if I moved, I would be sucked down, and if I tried to breathe, I'd swallow mud and it would get stuck in my throat and nostrils and I would… " His next words were a garbled mixture of English and Gaelic.

Ally turned and stared at Aiden. "This is the Stewart who wants you dead?" she asked. She sounded distraught.

"It has all the markings of one of his sadistic games," Aiden said quietly.

"But why Hamish?"

Aiden sighed and looked around at the empty landscape. "To get us out here on our own. He wants to separate us, just as Lorne said. And here we are. We must be careful, Ally."

She looked around as well, as if expecting to see Stewart waiting for them, but there was nothing. The rocky hills and the watery swamp were as barren. If Stewart was lurking somewhere, then he wasn't letting himself be seen. Ally gave a shiver.

"What is it?" Aiden put his arm around her, feeling her shiver again.

"There's something…a something in my head. A chill in my spine. Aiden, something doesn't feel right."

He tried to pick up on the unpleasantness Ally was feeling.

She made a whimpering noise. "Something… there's something coming. Oh God."

The surface of the boglach began to ripple. It was barely noticeable at first, and then more and more, until it was like a storm at sea. Only there was no wind to make a storm; the air around them was perfectly still.

Hamish, caught up in the midst of it, shrieked and started to topple over. Something flew overhead, blocking out the sun. The air was dry and hot, and Ally only had time to grasp hold of Aiden, and then they were both spinning.

His stomach threatened to spill its contents, and his head felt as if it might split open. It reminded him of when the Sorceress had sent him to sleep, back at the pet cemetery at Blackfriars Abbey. He wanted to shout out, but he had no voice. All he could do was hang on to Ally, try to keep her safe, and hope that they would survive whatever was to come.

And then there was nothing but heat filled darkness.

Chapter Nineteen

———◆———

IN THE SPINNING blackness and the chaos of the shifting world about her, Ally was aware of the passing of time. The sensation of days and nights moved by quickly until they turned into years. Soon she was far beyond her own lifespan, spinning backwards, always backwards.

She tried to hang on to consciousness, but it was a losing battle. Soon the darkness overwhelmed her, and she was lost to its oily warmth.

It was Aiden who woke her. He was shaking her, and at first she just wanted him to stop and leave her alone. But as his efforts grew in urgency, she forced her eyes open. Everything was blurred, but her other senses seemed to be working. It was quiet, and the air was musty and stale, as if she was locked up underground. The thought of that, of being deep in the earth, gave her a shot of adrenalin that brought her sharply awake.

There was a small metal cage bracketed into the wall, and inside it was the head of a blazing torch. Shadows flickered onto a low stone ceiling and smooth stone walls.

A tunnel, she decided. They were in some sort

of underground tunnel.

She opened her mouth to speak just as Aiden put his hand on her shoulder and squeezed a warning. She became aware of the voices then, rising from further down the stretch of tunnel far beyond the torch. A wild shout and then laugher. Drunken laughter. Ally's eyes found Aiden's. She saw something in his expression that made her think he was resigned to whatever situation they now found themselves in. As if something he had been dreading had finally happened.

"Aiden?"

"We're back," he said. Seeing her confusion, he explained. "This is one of the tunnels under Blackfriars Abbey. This is the Hellfire Club 1808."

Ally blinked, trying to collect her wits. Maybe it would have been better if she had remained unconscious, because this didn't sound at all good. "How?"

"I don't know," he admitted. "Stewart sent Maggie back, to try to turn her against Lorne, but it didn't work. She saw that the man he is now isn't the one he was then. Nicholas didn't have to go through this as far as I know, though he was in the Dark World, which may have been worse." He cleared his throat. "It's my turn now, it seems. I had a feeling it would happen. I just wasn't sure when."

Ally ignored his gloomy tone. "You think this is Stewart's work?"

"It seems the most likely explanation, given when it happened." Aiden considered the alternatives. "It could be the Sorceress, I suppose. She has threatened to make me confront my past, and recently managed to get inside my head in a way she never had before."

"Why on earth would she do this?"

He sighed and rubbed a hand over his face, and suddenly big, strong Aiden looked very vulnerable. "It is a game to her. She says she wants to make us better men, but instead of using simple means, she manipulates us for her own pleasure. I admit that it was our fault in the beginning, allowing the Destroyer to run free, but now she has us chasing after Stewart. His escape had nothing to do with us, and sometimes I wonder if she is simply trying to avoid blame."

"She sounds charming," Ally said sarcastically, and stared at him. "I don't know everything about your past, Aiden, but I know you are a good man. I've known plenty of bad, and you're not like them. You are loyal to your friends, and you love your dog." She smiled. "And you helped me when you didn't really need to. You were invisible in my cottage, for God's sake! Imagine how you could have taken advantage of that situation. But you didn't. You were always thoughtful and polite. No, Aiden, I'm sorry. I don't know what your so-called Sorceress is on about."

His dark eyes fixed on hers, reflecting back the torch flame. Something softened in his face, making her heart beat faster. She leaned forward, and felt his warm breath on her lips.

Their kiss was brief, barely a kiss at all. Just a touch of skin on skin. It wasn't enough, not nearly, but the voices in the tunnel grew louder, and they broke apart. It was the Hellfire Club and they were getting closer, and it sounded disturbingly as if they were hunting something. Or someone.

And Ally realised that the someone they were hunting might be them.

"Stay behind me," Aiden said. "Remember, these men are dangerous. Stupid and drunk and dangerous. They're not the men you met before."

"I'm not afraid," she said, struggling to her feet.

Aiden turned and looked at her, and there was none of the usual good humour or laughter in his eyes. "You should be, Ally. They may not be evil, but their casual disregard for others puts you at greater risk than you realise."

A chill went through her, but there was no time to respond, because the next moment Loki came bounding down the tunnel, made that odd howling noise, and leapt up at Aiden. He caught him, turned him around and put him down again next to Ally. "Stay," he commanded.

The dog was excited, but Ally caught hold of his scruff and held him as best she could. She struggled to get her head around the idea that this Loki was not the one she knew. He felt the same and looked the same. He even sounded the same.

Aiden stepped into the centre of the tunnel just as two men came striding through the darkness and into the flicking red torch light. Their expressions were gleeful.

She recognised them as Lorne and Nicholas, and yet they looked like different versions of the men she'd met earlier. Evil twins. Lorne's white shirt hung open at the throat. His dark hair fell in loose waves about his face, and his blue eyes gleamed red with the reflection of the torch fire. He staggered as he came to a stop, drunk but not showing it overly much.

Beside him, Nicholas was very drunk, and had difficulty walking at all. He leaned hard against the wall of the tunnel. He giggled to himself, and Ally noticed that the scar on his cheek was dark red, as though it had not yet fully healed.

"Well well, who have we here?" Lorne demanded. His eyes found Ally half hidden behind Aiden, and something in his gaze made her squirm inside. No, this most certainly wasn't the Lorne she had met. This wasn't him at all.

He tried to get around Aiden, but his balance betrayed him, and Aiden easily blocked his way.

"What are you doing down here?" Aiden asked in a reasonable voice. "There's more fun to be had up in the crypt."

Lorne pulled a face. "Your hound took off. He must have been following your scent. We followed him."

"Besides, the women there aren't any fun," Nicholas muttered. "They're asleep, and when we tried to wake them up, they got nasty."

"I'll fetch my whip. That will wake them up." Aiden sounded as if he meant it.

Ally bit her lip, reminding herself that Aiden had changed too. Besides, there had been a warm ripple of humour in his voice, as if it was a joke and not to be taken seriously.

Lorne and Nicholas now discussed the matter in low voices. Nicholas broke out in drunken chuckles every now and then with fresh ideas of pleasure and pain. They looked ridiculous, really, and Ally asked herself again whether she should really be afraid of them.

"Very well, fetch it then, shall we? Oh, and bring your friend," Lorne said. Something about the ice in his eyes sent a chill through her heart. No, this was serious, very serious, and she should be afraid.

Aiden glanced over his shoulder at Ally. "Why do you need her?" She read the warning and concern in his eyes.

"Have you forgotten? We are going to call up the demon, Sutcliffe," Lorne said with heavy patience, as if he was talking to a child. "Today's the big day. The grand finale of tonight's revelries. It may want something to feast upon when it arrives."

Nicholas laughed and gave a shout, and then they were heading back the way they'd come, weaving and stumbling against the walls. Loki gave a howl, but Ally hung on to him. Aiden waited until they were some steps ahead before turning to her.

"I think I know what this is about," he said. "This is the Sorceress's doing, not Stewart, or at least I believe so. She wants me to do what I should have done two hundred years ago. She wants me to stop Lorne from summoning the demon."

Ally looked at him curiously and more than a

little doubtfully. "Can you do it, Aiden? Is that even possible? Isn't the past already set?"

There was a spark of determination in Aiden's eyes. "I don't know if this is real or simply an illusion. A test. This is exactly the sort of thing the witch likes to throw at us. But regardless, I have to try. The alternative is unacceptable. And with you here, Ally…" He swallowed. "You've given me all the incentive I need."

"Can we do it again?" she asked suddenly.

His eyebrow lifted. "Do what again?"

"Kiss."

He smiled broadly and his arm came around her, hand on her hip, and he bent his head over hers.

"My pleasure," he said as his mouth came down over hers.

Ally felt the warmth of his lips, the brush of his tongue against her skin, and before she knew it, they were full on necking. She could have stayed there forever, and might well have done, had Loki not jerked her arm so that she released him, and he took off down the tunnel.

She gasped, pulling away, and Aiden stepped back, looking as dazed as she. For a moment, they simply looked at each other.

Something in her heart said, "Yes, he's the one," despite her head shaking with amazement and derision. Because how could she possibly know?

And yet she did.

Chapter Twenty

THE CRYPT HADN'T changed. Aiden wasn't sure why he thought it might have. He was in the past, after all. His past. Being here, seeing his friends, it was a shock, really. They had changed so much, he had changed, and this felt very wrong.

He held Ally's hand. Her auburn hair caught the light from the flaring torches as she looked all about her. He tried to see the crypt through her eyes, as one who had never been here before. Columns held up the vaulted ceiling, fires burned in braziers on the tiled floor to keep the place warm and drive off some of the damp. The women Nicholas had mentioned were asleep on a pile of cushions, dressed in garish and revealing costumes.

Aiden felt ashamed—ashamed of his stupid behaviour, reckless and ridiculous, dressed up in a monk's costume and wielding a whip. It had been harmless fun at first, a way to pass the time because they all seemed to have a great deal of that. But then it had changed, grown darker. With a growing sense of dread, he realised he was about to witness that transition.

He looked over at Lorne and Nicholas. They were bending over something by the raised dais and the chair that Lorne had dragged down from the house. It had the appearance of a throne, and as Lorne considered himself King of the Hell-fire Club, it had seemed appropriate. Aiden still remembered their laughter at their nonsense, before everything turned so dark and dangerous. And real.

He moved closer, Ally in tow, and saw the two men staring at a stone tablet. A shudder went through him. It was very old and covered in runes. He remembered the day the Egyptian had given it to them, his wizened face inscrutable as Lorne handed over the money. Now Lorne unrolled a piece of parchment, making a meal of it because of his precarious state.

"Sutcliffe!" Lorne bellowed, before turning and seeing his friend right there. His blue eyes widened comically.

"What the devil are you doing?" Aiden asked, although he knew very well. He thought that was what he had said two hundred years ago, so he may as well follow the script for now. He crouched down on his haunches.

"Not a devil, a demon. We're calling it up from hell," Nicholas said with another of those annoying giggles. "We're going to teach it to sing and frighten people. I want it to pay a visit to my parents, and Lorne wants it to bring back his grandmother so that he can tell her what he really thought of her."

It sounded amusing enough, payback for the two men's miserable pasts. Aiden remembered thinking he would send the demon off to visit his father, and hope the old bastard finally dropped dead from fright. Neither of his friends had believed anything would actually happen, but Aiden had felt something wasn't right. Now he knew the truth, and he needed to stop them. He needed to say the words he should have spoken two hundred years ago.

"I have a bad feeling about this," he began.

The two drunken fools stared at him as if he was speaking French. "Oh, come now. It's just a bit of fun!" Nicholas burst out.

Aiden closed his eyes and took a deep breath. I had a bad feeling when we did this, but I didn't tell you. I thought you wouldn't listen to me, so I stayed silent. I let you do it and people died. It's my fault.

"I don't think we should do this, Lorne. Just hear me out for a moment…"

Nicholas snorted. "When have you ever said no to some fun, Sutcliffe? And where's your whip?" He frowned at him, bleary-eyed, as if just now realising that Aiden looked different.

"Will you listen to me?" Aiden's frustration grew. "What you're doing is dangerous. It's not fun; it's evil. Demons cannot be controlled by the likes of us. It will kill people and destroy our lives. You don't realise how—"

Lorne's brilliant blue eyes were cloudy from drink and lack of sleep. They had been down in the crypt for days, Aiden remembered. It certainly hadn't helped their thinking.

"We talked about this," his friend said with jaded patience. "We need this. We need something to happen. The Hellfire Club has become boring. We've done everything we can, and no one stops us. No one cares. I want them to care. I want to show them."

"Show them?" Aiden was surprised he had forgotten this part of Lorne's personality. "Show them what? That you are as bad as people say? Is that what you want to show them? Why?"

"Why?" Lorne mocked. He turned to Darlington. "Why?"

"Because we can," Nicholas said. "Our tame demon will do whatever we tell it. We'll be able to make people listen to us, show them that... that we're not to be trifled with."

Aiden threw back his head in frustration. "No! Did you not hear me? This is no tame demon you are summoning. You will have no say over its actions. It's a trap, Lorne. You are falling into a trap. This has all been arranged by a man who hates you. He wants to destroy you in a way that will tear you apart. He wants to take you away from those you love."

He was starting to sound desperate, and, as he had always feared, they weren't listening to him. Lorne would do as he willed, and Darlington would follow along.

He took a deep breath and tried again. "Pretend for a moment that this spell actually works. If man could so easily control demons, why aren't they everywhere, doing our bidding? What if the spell works, but you can't control it? What then? It wreaks havoc and death, all of which will be our fault. Both of you are like brothers to me. More than brothers. I don't want you to live with this foolishness. You will regret it. We all will."

They were staring at him. He had them. He could feel it. They were listening to him.

Lorne opened his mouth to respond, doubt visible in his eyes.

Then there was a crash as the door to the crypt slammed open and someone charged down the stairs, all noise and impatience.

"Marquis! Are you really going to listen to this stupid man? You have the chance to make your mark. To bring a demon into your world. Who would dare defy a man capable of that? Do it now."

Aiden's blood froze. A small hand pressed into his shoulder, and a warm body leaned against his back. Ally. "Is that Stewart?" she breathed. "I thought he'd be bigger."

Stewart trotted into the crypt, the fires reflecting off his glasses. Ally was right. He looked anything but the budding master of the universe he claimed to be. That someone who looked so inoffensive should be so evil still surprised Aiden. Lorne and Nicholas seemed completely bewildered by Stewart's arrival, but then they didn't know who he was. Not yet.

"How dare you!" Lorne roared in all his aristocratic indignation. "Get out. This place is not for the likes of you."

Stewart cocked his head to one side. "Dear me,"

he murmured. "What a truly awful man you are."

The stunned silence lasted long enough for him to cast his eyes around at the others. When he came to Ally, the sudden stiffening of his body, and the smile on his lips, suggested he was surprised to see her here. Surprised but pleased.

"Ah, Miss MacDonald-Ellis," he purred. "How delightful to meet you again. It has been a while, hasn't it? How is your dear father?"

"I don't know you," Ally said stubbornly. Her hand slid into Aiden's and held tight.

Stewart chuckled, and his face changed in the flickering light, shifting, darkening. Ally gasped as if she recognised that face. A moment later, Stewart was himself again.

"Ari," she whispered. "How can you be here?"

"I can be anyone I want to be," Stewart retorted arrogantly. "And anywhere."

His gaze dropped to her hand, held fast in Aiden's, and he seemed to ponder them for a moment.

Despite his posturing, Stewart was genuinely surprised to see Ally here. Which meant it had to be the Sorceress who was at play here. The witchy woman wasn't to be trusted, but if it came to a choice between her and Stewart, Aiden would always choose her.

———◆———

Ally felt physically ill. Ari, the man she had loathed and feared for so long, the so-called guru who had come to her father's house and held him under his sway, who had frightened her with his intense stare and dark pronouncements, was Stewart. And here he stood before her now, smiling as if butter wouldn't melt in his mouth.

"How is your father?" he asked pleasantly, as if they were taking tea in a drawing room somewhere. "You didn't answer me before."

"I don't know. We don't talk very much. You put a stop to that." She tried to sound as cool about the situation as him, but was struggling to manage it.

Stewart chuckled. "Yes, I did, didn't I? He was afraid of you, you know." He tipped his head to one side. "He should have been in awe, but he wasn't strong enough to cope with the truth. He just wanted to take his drugs and drink his wine and sleep with his women." His gaze slid to Lorne and gave a little cough. "Sound like someone we know, hmm?"

"Get out of here," Lorne said again, his voice low and deadly. This shadow of the past may not know what was going on, but he seemed to understand that Stewart was a threat.

Stewart ignored him. His eyes were focussed on Ally through his glasses. "Your time is coming," he said to her. "I did tell you that, remember? Be ready, my dear."

Ally trembled, and only Aiden's hand kept her upright. Stewart didn't so much vanish but fade, and a strange blue light began to surround them, growing stronger and brighter, humming with power.

She had seen ghosts, spoken to them, and some had been very frightening, but this was outside her experience. The feeling of potency coming through the blue light made her tremble, and it was all she could do to cling to Aiden and watch.

"Gentlemen."

The voice made the hairs stand up on Ally's arms. A woman floated above the stone flags on the floor, her red hair weaving about her like Medusa's snakes. Her blue eyes were as dazzling as sapphires, and just as hard. For a moment, Ally couldn't move. Then she realised it was the force emanating from the woman that made it difficult to move, let alone think.

This was the Sorceress—there was no one else it could be.

"Madam." Aiden's voice sounded strained.

"I see Stewart has scurried away like the rat he is."

"He can't have gone far," Aiden suggested, hoping it was true.

"He's gone from this world," the Sorceress replied. "But never fear, we will have him yet. Soon. Be patient. If he is a rat, then Lorne is the cheese that will tempt him toward the trap."

When there was no response from his two friends, Aiden looked back at them. They were crouched, unmoving, unaware it seemed, locked in a moment from which he had long ago moved on. As he had thought, this whole flashback had been for his benefit.

As if she had read his mind, her azure blue eyes fastened onto him. Something in them shifted, a tail vanishing into a vast ocean. "I knew you were capable of doing the right thing, my lord. Now you believe it too."

He swallowed. She sounded pleased and proud, like a parent, and much to his surprise, it moved him more than he imagined it would.

"Have we finished here?" he asked, his voice low and a little shaky. "I want to take Ally home."

But where was home? Before he could begin to fathom the answer to that, the Sorceress laughed. It wasn't a sound he heard very often and not one he wanted to hear again.

"Yes, you can go, Aiden. For now. Bring me Stewart. You and your friends must show me what you are made of. I must see and believe that my efforts have not been wasted."

"Madam," he whispered, not sure what else he could say. Besides, she had already turned her attention to Ally.

"Ally," the Sorceress murmured. Then, louder, "You must be ready too. The time is coming. The end of days. Remember where your loyalties lie."

"My loyalties?"

"Stewart frightened you, didn't he? You ran away. Well, you might believe you have escaped his grasp, but his hold over you is stronger than you think. Be warned; he will not relinquish it easily."

Ally felt sick at the thought, but at the same time, she could not believe that Stewart had any hold over her, not any longer. But the Sorceress was right in a manner of speaking. Ally had run away from the commune because of Stewart, or Ari as he was known at the time. If he was so strong and she was so important to him, he would have stopped her, surely?

When she looked up again, the Sorceress was fading.

"Go back down the tunnel. The portal there will return you to Moyle. Be ready, my lord."

And then she was gone.

Aiden put his arms around Ally. They stood in silence for a moment, taking comfort from each other.

"Come," Aiden said, looking into her eyes, comforting and protective. "We must get back."

He took her hand in his, and the two set off together.

Chapter Twenty-One

THEY WALKED IN silence back the way they had come. The torch light flickered, causing the shadows to dance about them.

"I was right," Aiden said, his expression grim. "It was a test."

Ally turned to look up at him. "She wants to see how much you've all changed," she agreed. "And whether you can prove yourselves."

"Even if we die trying?" He raised his eyebrows. There was no humour in his voice.

"I don't think death is the point," Ally said dryly. "Perhaps death means nothing to her. It's just another realm. She isn't mortal."

"Then what is the point?" Aiden ducked his head slightly, keeping an eye on the height of the ceiling. "Lorne and Maggie are having a baby. Nicholas and Linny are in love. If we have to leave and return to the past... I've read the history books. It's a mystery when it comes to our deaths, but the best guess is we died in a fire set by the villagers. I understand what we did back then was wrong, but if she has taken the time to make us better people, to let us experience better lives, only to throw us to the wolves once our usefulness is at an end… then the point can only be cruelty."

Ally thought a moment. "When I left home and came to Moyle, I thought I could escape my past. But I haven't. It's followed me here. Maybe you can never truly escape. Sooner or later you have to face it, and do what you believe is right. That's all any of us can do. I don't know if she's done all of this with the expectation of taking it all away, but I think she sees a bigger picture than either of us possibly can. You have to have faith, I guess."

Aiden's expression softened into a smile.

They reached the part of the tunnel where they had arrived. Ally realised she couldn't see beyond where they stood. There was a dark mass there, moving in a slow spiral motion. The power of it made her body tremble. Aiden's fingers tightened on hers.

"Come on then. Forward," he said bravely.

They stepped into the portal, and that awful, sickening sensation began.

———◆———

Aiden was eight years old. He had told Essie to go and now he had changed his mind. With a cry he jumped up from his bed and ran out of the door and along the corridor. The man that was Aiden knew it was pointless, that it was too late. Essie had gone. But the boy Aiden still held hope.

The door to Essie's room was ajar and he pushed it open and… she was there!

When had the cold hard facts given way to this long held dream? He wasn't sure, but his heart lifted with joy as she turned to him, surprised by his sudden entrance, and then huffing out a breath as he ran into her arms.

"You're here! You didn't go!" he shouted.

She tightened her grip on him, holding him tight.

"I'm sorry, Essie. I'm sorry."

"Hush, my boy. Listen to me," she said. "I know it will be so hard for you when I am gone. Your mother only cares for you when there are visitors to parade you in front of, and your father is never satisfied no matter how hard you try to please. But, Aiden, never forget how much I love you and how proud I am of you."

Now he knew then that this was just a dream, that reality hadn't changed after all, and the life stretching before him would be difficult, and no matter how he strived he would receive no thanks from a mother too concerned with her own place in society, and a father who wanted his son to be just as brutal as him. It would turn him into the sort of man who stood silent while his friends caused bedlam for their own amusement.

He wished he could have had one last meeting with Essie. He wished he could have found her, safe, somewhere in Grenada, and told her how much she meant to him.

The past spun away again.

And Aiden blinked up at the sky.

He was lying on his back, with a perfect view of the heavy grey clouds that were gathering above. A fat drop of rain hit him on the nose and he blinked and rolled to the side. There was Ally. And she was real, and he was more than grateful that he had met her. She stared back at him, her green eyes a little lost as she adjusted to being back. The freckles on her nose stood out against her pallor, and a pink flush coloured her cheeks.

He had kissed her. Twice. Now he wanted to do it again. But before he could, she winced and rubbed her stomach.

"I don't want to go through that again, thank you very much."

He reached out and smoothed a strand of her hair from her temple, lingering to brush his fingertips over her soft skin. He couldn't seem to look away.

"I'm sorry," he said.

"What for?" Her hand reached up to clasp his. "This isn't your fault."

"You can see that it is. Three bored, stupid men. We started this."

"Stewart started it. This is all about him. He is like a spider spinning an enormous web, and we're caught in his sticky strands, struggling and all the time wondering when he'll leave the shadows and come crawling down the web to feed."

It sounded awful, yet absolutely correct. Stewart's insane hatred of Lorne had driven him to start his web, his need to make the Marquis hurt as he had been hurt. And although Aiden knew Lorne wasn't innocent, at least he had striven to change. He was no longer the man he had been. Could Stewart say the same? Lorne didn't deserve whatever horrible fate Stewart had in store for him.

Ally's soft hand cupped his bristly cheek. Aiden met those green eyes, and then she leaned in and kissed him. Her mouth was warm, and he groaned and deepened the kiss, sliding his tongue in, tasting her, exploring. She made a sound of pleasure, her other hand resting on his nape, fingers sliding through his short hair. His hands found their way down her back, to her waist, and then further, closing over the rounded cheeks of her bottom.

Ally wriggled in closer to him, deliberately fitting herself to him, and he ached. He was hard, getting harder, and he lost himself in the sensation of her. He wanted her, and she seemed to want him. Just for a moment, it felt like a perfect idea to take her. He hadn't had a woman in, well, two hundred years, and he wanted this one. Not just because it had been a long time, but because it was Ally. And he was beginning to think that this woman was special.

"Ahem."

The sound brought Aiden out of the moment. Not straight away, but after the second ahem, the toe of a boot nudged his shoulder. He turned abruptly, blinking up, thinking… well, he wasn't sure what he was thinking. Anything could have crept up on them while they had been so pleasantly engaged, and he cursed himself for it.

Hamish Morison stood looking down at them with a frown. Mud streaked his face and jeans, and his once pristine Moyle sweater was soaked and filthy.

"Hamish!" Ally struggled up to her feet, using Aiden's body to steady herself. "Oh, you're alive! We thought... oh Hamish, I'm so glad."

Hamish took her willingly in his arms, and Aiden guessed from the look on the young man's face that Hamish had a small crush on her. Of course he did. Who wouldn't? Hamish grinned as she stepped back. Ally gazed at him as if she couldn't believe he was still alive.

"What happened?" she asked.

As Aiden got to his feet, Hamish explained how a man calling himself Mr Stewart had appeared out of nowhere and said he was here to help with Ally's garments. He seemed genuine and pleasant, and appeared to know all about her, so Hamish had taken him at his word. He was a polite boy and couldn't refuse helping out.

"The next thing I knew I was standing in the boglach. Mr Stewart told me not to move, that I would sink if I did, and the mud would fill up my mouth and nose and..." He swallowed and shook his head, as if to shake off the horrible images. "Then you came and suddenly there were those strange waves, and I knew I was going to die."

"But you didn't," Ally said.

"No," Hamish agreed. "I didn't." He looked surprised and rather pleased. He reached out as if to hug Ally again, and then caught Aiden's eye and didn't.

"What happened to you after the waves?" Ally asked.

"I..." He looked confused and dragged his hands through his red hair, dislodging some mud and rotten leaf matter. "There was a ghostly woman. Or at least I think she was. She came with a blue light around her, and when she spoke I felt myself rising up out of the boglach. She didn't touch me, but she lifted me… somehow." He looked sheepish, as if he wasn't sure they would believe him. "I know it sounds crazy, but—"

"I've met that woman too," Ally reassured him. "She is a sort of friend of Lord Sutcliffe here. A good friend. I hope." All the same, she gave Aiden a doubtful glance. "At least you're safe," she added firmly, "that's the main thing."

Hamish gave Aiden an uncertain look, as if his being friends with the Sorceress made him someone Hamish preferred not to deal with. Aiden didn't blame him.

"I think you should go to your aunt's cottage and let her know you're fine," Ally said firmly. "Take my scooter. Aiden and I will take your cart and fetch the knitwear and take it to the hotel. Tell your aunt that, won't you, Hamish? She should still come to the hotel to set up shop. We need to be ready by tomorrow evening when the ceilidh begins."

Her smile was a little shaky, but Hamish didn't seem to notice. Even if he did, he wasn't going to ask any more questions after what they'd been through. He was simply relieved to get away from this place alive. Another hug from Ally, and he set off at a quick lope.

Ally and Aiden made their way to the cart, but before they reached it, the rain began to fall.

"The weather here is… interesting," Aiden said,

looking up at the sky. It was even greyer than it had been before, and there seemed to be a number of clouds gathering. Was another storm on the way? It seemed appropriate somehow now that they were approaching the end of their quest.

"I think it's just a passing shower," said Ally, but frowned as if she wasn't sure. "We can shelter in my cottage until it passes. Wayward will be glad to see us."

"You, perhaps."

Aiden thought of Loki. He hoped his companion was safe with the others, and assumed he was getting very spoilt. What would become of Loki at the end of this journey? Would the Sorceress send the dog back to the past as well, or simply set him loose somewhere?

There were too many questions. Always too many. Best to take things one step at a time. The Sorceress was here with them, and that was somewhat comforting, but Stewart had more in store for them. Aiden was sure of it.

Chapter Twenty-Two

THE COTTAGE WAS as they'd left it, and Wayward was desperate for food, although Ally was sure she couldn't be that hungry. After she had tended to the cat, she sent Aiden to the shower while she changed into dry clothing. Because there was nothing here that would fit Aiden, she suggested he sit by the fire she lit, wrapped up in one of her knitted rugs while his clothes dried.

He didn't protest, and was soon staring into the flames, hunched over. He probably had a lot on his mind; they both did. There were the kisses they had shared, of course, but she wasn't going to think about them. Not yet, anyway.

The rain was now so heavy it was almost impossible to see beyond the gate. Definitely not a Scottish mist, more like a tropical downpour, but cold. The light was fading too. It would be dark soon. It didn't seem as if they'd be going anywhere tonight.

Ally found the number of the hotel on her mobile phone, glad to see there was still a signal, and after the usual irritation of dealing with

Mrs Shaw on reception, got through to Lorne's suite. She handed the phone to Aiden so he could explain what had happened while she went to heat up some soup from the freezer. She wasn't as hungry as Wayward pretended to be, but she needed to eat and she was sure that Aiden did as well.

Aiden's voice was too low to hear properly, apart from a word or two. While she dealt with their meal, she thought about the remaining garments that needed to be taken to the hotel. Most were stored in the cottage of one of the women who lived close to the town. These remaining items were an exclusive collection. More work had gone into them, and the designs were amazing. The prices would reflect that. Ally knew that some of the guests would buy gloves or a scarf or even a sweater to take home with them, but others would look at these special one-off pieces and be willing to pay a great deal more to own one.

Her thoughts slipped away from the shop and the business, everything that had mattered to her for the past year. Now she found herself trying to come to grips with what had happened at the boglach. Journeying back through time to the Hellfire Club, seeing Aiden's friends so different to how they were now. Aiden trying to change the past, and the Sorceress smiling at him as if he was her favourite pet project.

She'd learned Stewart was Ari, and he'd spoken of Ally as if he had some master plan involving what was to come tomorrow night. Ally didn't know what to make of any of it. She was afraid. If she allowed herself to consider the ramifications, her thoughts would spiral somewhere very dark.

She needed to stay calm, for her sake and Aiden's.

Ally stopped. When had Aiden Sutcliffe become so important to her? Just remembering that mad moment by the marsh, his mouth on hers, his body pressed to hers, had her hot and bothered in a way she had never been before.

She carried the soup over to the fire and set the tray down on the coffee table. This wasn't a night for formal dining, especially with Aiden swathed in a colourful knitted rug. She pressed her lips tight. It probably wasn't the time to be laughing at him, either.

He had finished his call and once again stared into the fire. Something about the stiff set of his shoulders, the way his hands clenched in his lap, made her think he was reliving those moments in the past with his friends. Or perhaps he was thinking of a future they may not have.

They ate in silence, but Ally had questions she needed answers to, and they had barely finished when she spoke.

"Why does Ari… I mean Stewart… Why does he hate Lorne so much?"

Aiden looked over at her, his dark eyes filled with dancing orange flames. "Stewart's real name is Noakes, and his mother, Mrs Noakes, was Lorne's nursemaid. Noakes was her bastard son, a miserable little runt. We didn't even remember him until he reminded us. He hates Lorne because his own mother loved Lorne more than him.

"And when we called the Destroyer into the world, one of his first victims was Mrs Noakes. So he hates Lorne for that too. It was the Egyptian who gave us the runes to bring the Destroyer into the world, and once Mrs Noakes was dead, the Egyptian took her son away with him as a sort of apprentice. He trained him, but also abused him. Eventually, Noakes killed him and took his place. I imagine that was where the role of Ari the guru came from. So Noakes also hates Lorne for his suffering at the Egyptian's hands."

Ally considered his words. "That's a lot of hate."

"And it's only grown over the centuries. He's been consumed by it. Rotten to the core."

Ally could imagine that. It explained Stewart, in a way. Something occurred to her, though, something that may not have occurred to anyone else, because of her particular realm of experience.

"If Noakes loved his mother so much, why hasn't he brought her back to life? He's obviously a very powerful man or, well, whatever he is. Why hasn't he used those powers when it comes to his mother, Aiden?"

She could see he didn't know. That it had never even occurred to him.

"I'm just speculating," Ally continued, raising her voice above the rain, "but perhaps he knows she wouldn't approve of what he's doing. He wants to avenge her, but he's aware she would not agree with him, so he isn't giving her the chance to have her say."

Aiden's frown softened into a smile. "That could well be so. But how does it help us?"

"I'm not sure yet. But I wonder…" She hesitated, because what she was about to say now was no simple task, and rather frightening to her. "I wonder if I could call up Mrs Noakes? Bring her spirit into this world. If I'm right, and her son so desperately wants her love and approval, she might be the key to stopping him. Or at least throwing him off balance."

Aiden's short hair had dried into a spikey mess and she could see one bare broad, muscled shoulder where the rug had slipped down. He watched her now with his intense dark eyes.

"Can you do that?" he asked her. "Bring Mrs Noakes back?"

"I don't know if I can. Normally, the spirits find me, not the other way around. However…"

He nodded, waiting for more. Ally took a breath.

"Before I came to Moyle, I was practising scrying in order to help lost souls. Do you know what 'scrying' is?"

Aiden shook his head. At least he hadn't laughed at her outright, but then she would not expect Aiden to do that. He was even more acquainted with the world of the supernatural than she was. She gathered her thoughts.

"You can use any polished surface, really, but I used a black mirror. Some people will run water down over its surface to blur the reflections. I had to stop using it because… it felt uncomfortable. I thought it might be easier to speak to a spirit through the mirror, but it's supposed to also be capable of initiating contact as well."

"But you've never tried?"

"I wanted to put all of that behind me when I came to Moyle."

She didn't tell him about the feeling she'd had that Ari was always behind the mirror somewhere, watching her, tracking her movements.

"I was sure I'd given the mirror away before I moved, but somehow it ended up in my luggage when I moved. I considered throwing it away, but for now I've felt as if it was safer for me if I keep an eye on it, so it's covered up, in my bedroom."

"It sounds dangerous," Aiden said softly. "Would you be putting yourself in danger, Ally?"

His care of her was unexpectedly sweet. "We're all in danger," she reminded him, "and we need to follow every possible lead if we're going to defeat Stewart."

Aiden agreed. "Do you want to wait until we're with the others?"

"I think it would be better if I did it here. I could try it now, if you like."

She could see he was conflicted. She had seen he was perfectly capable of dealing with most things, but childhood traumas tended to linger and shape one's personality, as she knew all too well.

"I'd better get dressed then," he said.

Ally opened her mouth, then bit her lip. But he must have read her thoughts, because a smile tipped the corners of his mouth and his eyes warmed with something she didn't dare explore right now.

Instead, she said, "Yes. I'll get your clothes from the drier."

She left them for him on the sofa and went through to her bedroom where the mirror was. It rested against the wall, the ornate frame and dark glass covered by a cloth. It would probably be better to do this in the lounge, so she carried it carefully into the other room.

Aiden was just pulling on his shirt and looked sexy as hell as he glanced in her direction. Her body heated in a way it hadn't done for a long time. Desire, need, and more than that. They had a connection, and she wondered what that meant, and whether they would have a chance to explore it further.

Perhaps, but first things first.

She set the mirror down against the back of a chair, then turned off the overhead light. The soft shadows from the fire and a lamp over in the kitchen were just what she needed. When she turned to Aiden again, he was standing with his arms crossed, watching her intently.

"I'll just get comfortable. If you sit there behind me, and don't speak unless you have to. It might take a little while to, uh…" She shrugged.

"To get through to her," Aiden said dryly. "Not like a mobile phone call, I suppose?"

"Not quite." And, as she had said earlier, she had never contacted anyone from her end before. They always contacted her. But she understood how it was supposed to be done. She smiled and turned to the mirror. It was time to see if she had what it took to do this. She really hoped the prickly sensation that Ari was watching her from behind the veil would not return. But needs must, as they say...

The black polished surface looked soft in the muted light, almost as if her fingers could reach inside. In a way, it was a doorway, a portal, and even if her hand could not pass through, her mind could.

Ally settled down in front of the mirror and straightened her back. She took some deep breaths, gaze fixed on the dark surface. The fire flickered at the corner of her eye, but she ignored it, letting herself drift deeper and deeper into the void that lay before her.

"Mrs Noakes," she whispered, or thought she did. Perhaps the words in her head never actually reached her lips. "We need to speak to you. About your son. About the one you treated like a son. You loved Lorne, didn't you? You'd want to help him. We need your help, Mrs Noakes. Mrs Noakes."

The chant went on and on in a loop, reaching out into nothingness. Ally wasn't sure how long she sat there. At last, the dark clouds in the mirror began to swirl. She didn't actually lean forward, but it felt as if she did, and then she was falling. It wasn't the same as when she had been spun through time. This was a softer sensation, as if she was floating. Drifting.

At first, there was nothing at all, only silence and the occasional brush against her skin like gentle fingers. She could smell flowers, sweet and strong, and a warm humid breeze stirred her hair.

"Aiden? Oh, Aiden!" The voice was a woman's, with a sing song accent.

"Mrs Noakes?" Ally asked tentatively.

"Essie?" Aiden said at the same time

The shock in his voice was evident. He had moved from his seat and was now kneeling behind Ally, his hand on her shoulder and his breath warm on her cheek. "Essie, is that you?" There was an ache in his voice, as if his dearest wish was about to be granted.

Chapter Twenty-Three

THE RAIN HAD been heavy for some time now, and Lorne lay watching it from the sofa in their room. Maggie was tired, and had fallen asleep against him, and he hadn't wanted to wake her. So here he reclined, watching the rain, watching the night, with far too much time to think.

Maggie was heavy and warm in his arms, her curly hair tickling his nose. The baby, their baby, was taking all of her energy, she said, so that he could grow. She called the baby 'he' as if she already knew they had a son. Lorne wasn't so sure. The McNab sisters were strong willed, and this baby could just as easily be a girl.

Either outcome would be perfect. Maggie was perfect. Their life together could be perfect.

He shook his head. No, nothing was ever perfect, was it? They would argue. She would tell him he worried too much and was too bossy, and he would promise to take a step back, then continue to worry and be bossy. Because he didn't want to lose her.

Their time together was growing short, perhaps hours now. Soon it would be minutes. He didn't pretend to believe everything would turn out well, despite his desire for it to be so. In the end, he might be transported back to 1808 and Blackfriars Abbey, back to a life he could no longer contemplate without a shudder.

He'd been such a fool. A selfish idiot without understanding or care for the feelings of others. He had been injured as a child and therefore believed everyone else should feel his pain. Of course, he hadn't been all bad. He had his friends, the two men he loved like brothers, and Mrs Noakes, his nanny. She had been his mother, in a way, and yet it had been his love for her and her preference for him over her own son that had started all this trouble.

Love and hate. One fed off the other, it seemed. His love for Maggie and their baby, and his hate for Stewart, and Stewart's hatred for him, which now threatened Maggie.

He should never have summoned the Destroyer. The man he now was would not have done it. But then, if he hadn't called upon the demon and set this whole nightmare in motion, he would never have met Maggie. She wouldn't be here with him now. Their child would not be growing inside her. And yet so many people had died along the way... It was a conundrum.

"Lorne?" Maggie was awake; her warm brown eyes fixed on his face. How long had she been watching him? How much had she seen? Probably a great deal more than he wanted her to.

"Feeling better?" he asked, allowing her to sit

up. She pushed her hair aside and took a breath. The colour was back in her face, and there was a determined sparkle in her eyes he knew well.

"Better, but what about you? What's wrong? I know there's something. Talk to me."

He sighed. "I was thinking about the past. Regretting what I did, then wondering if I should regret something that brought me to you. Is it selfish of me to be thankful for that part of it? People have died, Maggie, and yet still I have you."

"My love," she murmured and reached to hold him.

For a time, they were silent, simply enjoying their closeness.

"What will we do if the Sorceress allows you to stay?" Maggie asked dreamily.

"I haven't thought," he admitted. "I haven't dared to."

"Then you should. We should. Did you want to go back to Blackfriars? Perhaps we can open it to the public." She laughed when she felt him stiffen. "The plebs can run their grubby hands all over your ancestral home."

"Very funny." He frowned in thought. "If we did, we'd have to do something with the place. I can't see us living there in solitary splendour." He stopped. "I suppose it hasn't fallen down? Last time we were there, it looked near to it."

"Well, we could go somewhere else. Some-where warm," she added, with a shiver and a glance outside at the rain. "Would you like that?"

"As long as it isn't Hell," he said dryly, and then

winced when she hit his arm. "My apologies. I don't know, Maggie. I haven't thought. So long as I am allowed to stay, and you and the baby are with me, nothing else really matters."

She stared at him a moment, then smiled, her lips trembling with emotion. "You're right," she agreed. "Nothing else matters."

He leaned in to kiss her, his desire rising. "Is it…?" he began, but she kissed him again, silencing his worry.

"Everything is just as it should be," she whispered. "Take me to bed."

He stood up, took her in his arms, and carried her to the bedroom. He wouldn't think about how long they had left, how this could well be the last time he caressed her and felt the joy of being with her.

"It'll be all right," Maggie whispered, reading his thoughts.

Lorne kissed her again before he closed the door. "Of course it will."

Chapter Twenty-Four

NICHOLAS HAD BEEN staring out of the window in their room. The rain was constant and heavy, falling into the darkness. Despite the weather, he could hear sounds in the hotel. When he'd ventured down to the lobby, he'd seen the pop-up shops Ally had been talking about beginning to take shape. The woman at reception didn't seem to think the festivities would be called off because of a "wee drop of rain."

He supposed if one waited for the sunshine on Moyle, nothing would ever happen.

Behind him, Linny was lying on the bed, replete, after a vigorous round of lovemaking. He still couldn't believe his luck. He had crossed two centuries chasing a monster, and in the process had found the woman of his dreams. What was even harder to believe was that she had wanted him back, especially when you considered the sort of man he was.

Had been, he reminded himself. He had changed.

Linny reminded him of that constantly; she would never have fallen in love with the old

Nicholas, the one who had done such terrible, selfish things. She loved the man he had become and for that he was forever grateful.

But with that gratitude came the very real fear that he would soon be separated from her forever.

"The witchy woman won't let that happen," Linny had said earlier, when he had suggested a less than perfect ending for them all. "I don't like her much, but she loves her Hellfire Club boys. No matter what she says, she won't send you back to stand trial, or let Stewart hurt you. Well, not mortally, anyway. I suspect she enjoys a bit of bloodshed, that one."

"Linny," he'd replied, "she isn't mortal. She doesn't have the same morals or feelings as we do. I'm not sure she even understands what human love is."

Linny looked stubborn. "Then why is she so keen on turning you three into better men?"

"I think it's something to do with her not wanting to be seen as a failure by Sigurd."

Linny snorted, as if she found that hard to believe. "When I sacrificed so much for Maggie, to see her succeed, to see her happy, it wasn't because I didn't want to be seen as a failure, Nicholas. It was because I loved her."

Nicholas had let the subject lapse, but he still had doubts that the Sorceress was capable of such feelings. He genuinely hoped she was because that would suggest she would spare them when the time came. That she would ensure that their lives were not cut short, not when they had finally made amends for their past.

Linny turned on her side; her long fair hair spread out behind her on the pillow. He let his gaze slide over her, the sweet face and slightly open mouth, those long dark eyelashes. When she was asleep, she looked innocent, but she had grown up tough. She would fight tooth and nail for him if she had to. But that would be a fight even she couldn't win.

Sometimes he imagined their lives together as a couple, but not very often. Best not to get caught up in wishful thinking. Then, if things went very wrong, it wouldn't hurt quite as much. But he knew that wasn't true. Of course it would hurt regardless. He would be destroyed. Death would be a welcome relief if they were destined to be parted.

And it was his sincere hope that he never return to the Dark World. He'd had quite enough of that living nightmare, thank you. He gave a shudder at the memory of those spinning cages and the black void that led to the Underworld. He would never forget the lingering scent of brimstone.

He did not want to leave the mortal world. He and Lorne would give anything to stay, and after seeing Aiden with Ally, he suspected he would too. They'd seemed very close, considering Aiden had been invisible for much of that time.

The thought made him snort a laugh.

"What?" Linny asked. She stretched lazily into wakefulness, watching him with half-closed eyes, a smile on her lips.

"I was just thinking about Aiden being invisible in Ally's cottage and what they got up to."

Linny's smile broadened. "Really? I can't imagine they got up to much, or…maybe I can. Kinky."

Nicholas climbed back into the bed at her feet, capturing her ankles in his hands, massaging them gently, his hands moved up over her calves. She leaned up on her elbows and ran her pink tongue over her bottom lip.

"Again?" she purred. "You're insatiable, my lord."

"You make me so," he murmured. Then, the words spilling out of him, "I shall miss this, if…"

She pulled away and sat up. "Nicholas, stop." She leaned forward, kneeling on the bed so that they were eye to eye. "I love you. It will be all right, understand? I know it will. You will stay and we will be together. There's so much here I want to show you, and we have years and years ahead of us."

He nodded and bowed his head, soothed despite his own misgivings. She reached out and cupped his chin, lifting his face so that he had to meet her eyes. "And I want you to see a specialist. A doctor," she added, when he looked blank. "For your leg."

He began to shake his head. He'd always believed his leg was punishment for the evil that he had done, but she had refused to accept that.

"You need to see someone, Nicholas. Medicine has changed so much. You could have your leg operated on. It may never be perfect, but it can be better. Imagine being without pain. You deserve to live your life without pain."

"Sometimes I wonder…"

"Please, stop punishing yourself." Her eyes were shining with tears now. "I hate seeing you in pain all the time."

Nicholas saw only love and the wish to help in Linny's gaze. He wondered what it would be like to be without that constant ache in his leg, where it had been broken all those years ago. But did he really deserve to be without the pain? He wasn't sure, but Linny wanted to help him, so he nodded.

"Very well. If I survive what comes next, and we are together, then I will see your specialist, my love."

She gave one of those ear-splitting shrieks and flung her arms around his neck. He tried not to wince, and then he was rolling with her on the bed, and soon he had forgotten everything else.

Chapter Twenty-Five

E SSIE WAS SPEAKING to him. There was no mistaking her melodious accent, and Aiden, despite all he had been through, struggled to believe that such a thing was possible.

"You are sad," she said. "You feel responsible for what happened to me."

"I was. I told you to go and…" His voice broke.

"You were a child. You were hurt. There is no blame in that, Aiden. There were others far more to blame than you. Your father and your mother, even me."

"You? Why you? It was never your fault."

The black mirror stared back at him, and he imagined he could see her face, her wide smile and gentle brown eyes.

He asked the question he had dreaded for so long. "What happened to you? Did my father… were you hurt?"

"He sold me. It was not a pleasant place. I did not live very long, which was probably a good thing. No, no, don't be sad. It is all over and long ago."

"I am so sorry, Essie. So sorry. Please forgive

me." He was choked with sadness and guilt, and tears ran down his cheeks. He could not remember the last time he had cried like this. Probably when he was eight.

"I know you are, love. I forgive you with all my heart. I want you to live a happy life, because you are a good man. It would please me if I knew you were happy, Aiden. Worrying about you is the only thing that has kept me from crossing over."

"Oh no, oh please, don't stay there. Essie, don't worry about me anymore, please. I am… I am fine." He took a deep breath. "You were the person I loved the most. You know that, don't you?"

"Like my own child," she whispered. "Be happy, Aiden. Make a life for yourself. Will you promise me that, my boy?"

"Yes. I promise, Essie."

There was a sigh that drifted into silence.

After a moment, Ally said, "She's gone."

Aiden nodded, even though Ally had her back to him. "She was everything to me," he said quietly. "My father owned her. He owned many more in Grenada, working them on his plantation as if the colour of their skin precluded them from having feelings. But he brought Essie home. I thought she was my friend but when I realised she was his mistress, I was angry and upset. My life would have been very different if she had stayed, but perhaps I deserved to be miserable, because her leaving was my fault. I threw a tantrum when I found them together and told her to go."

"She forgave you," Ally said gently. "I heard her say it. I'm glad you had that moment with her,

Aiden. I'm glad I made that possible."

He felt as though a poison had been drained from him. Essie had forgiven him, and now he felt hopeful, as if the worst was over. Although, of course, it wasn't.

They were silent for a moment, both lost in thought. "I don't think Mrs Noakes will come now," Ally said. "But at least some good came from this. It was good, wasn't it?"

She turned then to face him. She looked tired, as if the black mirror and Essie had drained her energy.

"Yes," he said, and managed a shaky smile. "Thank you, Ally. Thank you so much." He reached out and hauled her into his arms.

He hadn't meant to do more than hug her, but the sudden touch of their bodies caused an over-whelming need within him. His mouth fused on hers, firm and eager, and she responded just as eagerly. The passion that had been humming for days between them had become a pounding, raging, living force. Her hands clung to his biceps as she attacked his mouth, and he groaned, lifting his head so he could look her in the eyes.

"I want you," he said. "Do you want me?"

She did, but he needed her to say so. Remembering his stupid and irresponsible past, he had to make certain she knew what she was doing.

"Yes, I want you."

Then they were kissing again, without restraint. Aiden knew they needed this connection between them, this affirmation of life.

It didn't take long to undress. He touched her

bare skin as they resumed kissing and exploring one another. She was his perfect woman, soft and curved. He cupped her breasts, dipping his head to take a nipple in his mouth. She arched back in delight, clasping him to her. Aiden smiled against her skin. Perfect, too, in that she was enjoying this as much as him.

"I need a bed," he growled, and felt her laughter.

———◆———

Aiden was a large man, strong and handsome. The dark hair on his chest matched his head, and his cock was long and thick and eager. Ally would have looked longer, but he was already lifting her up in his arms and carrying her to the bedroom.

It had been so long since anyone had carried her, but Aiden did it easily. He tossed her onto the mattress and then he came down on her, holding her firm as they kissed. It was as if a dam had burst, their desire for each other now overwhelming.

She wrapped her legs around his waist and felt the nudge of him between them. Oh God, condoms. Did she have any? The thought brought her to her senses.

"Wait," she said breathlessly. "I think…"

She scrambled out from under him and over to the side of the bed. The drawers on the side table took some tugging to open; they had always jammed in wet weather. There it was. A present from a friend from Glasgow who had stayed a few months ago. They had been drinking whiskey and laughing about the sorry state of their love lives. The next week Ally had got a gift in the mail, a packet of novelty flavoured condoms.

She'd thrown them in the drawer, never expecting to have the opportunity to use them. Now she was very grateful to her friend's sense of humour.

Aiden eyed the packet in her hand. It occurred to her he may not know what they were, but when he took it from her and opened it up, taking out a single foil packet, she decided he did know.

"I've been watching a lot of television," he said, "but I may need some help."

Holding back a gurgle of laughter, she took it from him and did the work. He leaned forward, resting his brow against her head. "That feels good," he whispered. "It's been so long, and you are… I want you, Ally. Not for a moment, not for an hour. I want you to be with me for as long as I have left in this world."

She looked up at him, wide-eyed. Did she feel the same? She thought she did. And the idea that he may not be here very long, that Stewart may finish him, or her, or that he may be forced to leave regardless of the outcome, left an ache in her chest. But she wanted to make her commitment now, despite their uncertain future. She needed to.

"I want you too," she said. Her palm rubbed against the rough scratch of beard on his jaw. "More than I ever imagined I could want a man. I don't trust easily, Aiden, but I trust you."

A moment later, they were kissing again, and

he pressed against her warm body, seeking entry. She arched against him, moaning in pleasure, as lost in the moment as he. There was no need to think about the past or the future. Just the now, with them here together, Aiden and Ally.

Chapter Twenty-Six

ALLY WAS DOZING, sated. The two of them lay cuddled together in the cooling air. The cottage was cold, she realised, and she needed to stoke the fire and add some more fuel. It was still raining. She wasn't sure how long they'd be stuck here. Best to wait until it stopped before they set out.

She felt wonderfully relaxed. Her thoughts drifted to Aiden's encounter with the slave, Essie. She knew many of the wealthy families in England had traded in human beings, the ships landing in Africa to take on unwilling victims and then sailing on to the West Indies or America, before returning home with their hulls full of sugar or cotton. Aiden's family must have been one of those who'd acquired their fortune from such a disgraceful practice. She wondered if her own had done the same. She had never asked her father.

She was glad Aiden had the chance to make his peace with Essie. She had seen how much it meant to him, and could tell how much it meant to her.

Cold breath brushed over her face and Ally's eyes snapped open.

Someone loomed over the bed, peering down at her. Her ability to move, to scream, had abandoned her and she could only stare back. It was a middle-aged woman, her eyes piercing beneath unplucked brows and her hair scraped back beneath a white cap. She wore a simple dress, a neckerchief tied about her throat, and she twisted it with fingers whose knuckles had grown swollen from arthritis and hard work.

Ally had never seen her before.

The woman's gaze moved between Ally and Aiden and softened. This wasn't Essie; she knew that much. Could it be Mrs Noakes? She tried to sit up, but as soon as she moved, the woman was gone. Like Aiden blinking on and off, she'd been there one moment and gone the next. The bedroom was empty.

Just another spirit, she told herself. She should be used to their visits by now. Only she didn't get visits since she had arrived in Moyle.

The thought faded as Aiden's large form moved closer, warming her more than any fire. He nuzzled against her throat, his mouth warm and eager. "Want you," he murmured, and Ally put the strange experience out of her mind.

"Again?" she teased.

"Can't get enough," he said, surprised at his own admission.

"Neither can I," she admitted, feeling that heat of passion re-ignite.

His dark eyes shone as they met hers, and she

forgot all about wandering spirits as he took her in his arms.

———◆———

The knock on the door the next morning came as a surprise. Ally had collected the last of the finished garments, ready to bring them to the hotel. She certainly wasn't expecting visitors. After yesterday, she wasn't sure she wanted any.

Aiden was in the shower and Ally hesitated to open the door, wondering if she should call him first. Then she told herself that it was highly unlikely Stewart would turn up at her door for a visit. More probable that it was Mrs Morison, or one of the Hellfire Club boys, and—as they knocked again—she needed to answer.

It was a stranger, after all. A woman with a fluffy grey beanie pulled down over her hair and a black coat, with the fur-lined collar turned up. She had started to turn away, thinking there was no one home, but looked back once Ally opened the door.

For a moment, Ally was too stunned to do more than gawp. It was like looking into a mirror twenty years into the future.

Same green eyes, pointed chin, and small straight nose. Perhaps her face was more fine-boned than Ally's, and there was a sadness to the curve of her mouth.

"Hello Alison," she said in a soft Scottish accented voice.

"Mum?" Ally whispered.

It wasn't really a question, because she knew it was her. Seeing her now, though, in the midst of everything happening to her, threw her off-kilter.

"I'm here in Moyle with my husband," Maeve MacDonald said. "I…" She hesitated, and glanced past Ally into the cottage, as if wanting to be invited in, but not daring to ask. With a jolt, Ally remembered her manners.

"Come in," she said.

Maeve took off her coat, and Ally could see that she was delicately built, unlike Ally's more solid, curvy frame. When she removed her hat, it was obvious where Ally got her auburn hair from. There was an awkward silence.

"Would you like some tea? A coffee?" Ally asked, as her mother stood in the lounge, glancing about her. She had noticed the knitwear, bending in for a closer look.

"Is this you?" she asked with an upward glance and a smile.

"Some of it. There is a group of us. We have a pop-up shop at the hotel. Are you here for the ceilidh?"

Maeve brushed her fingers over the brightly patterned scarf, then sat down on the edge of the sofa. The warmth of the fire spread into the room and she seemed to be enjoying it.

"Yes. My husband fits out hotels, although he didn't do this one. He has contacts, though, and thought it would be a good idea to come along and meet some of the other guests. He's always networking. I wasn't sure whether to join him or not. I knew you were here, Alison, but I didn't know if you'd want to see me. It's been a long time."

It had been a long time. Ally had known her mother was still alive, although she did not know any details. But she could have found out. She could have gone knocking on her door. She hadn't. The woman who had walked out on her when she was a child had grown more distant as time went on—a stranger. Ally wasn't sure they had anything in common, and their shared memories were not ones she was keen to revisit.

Ally moved to the kitchen, boiling the kettle, preparing tea despite not having had an answer to her invitation. "How did you know I was here?"

"I was booking our visit to Moyle and your name came up. 'Bright young businesswoman putting Moyle on the map.'"

"So you didn't just come for your husband's business networking? Were you planning to kill two birds with one stone? Attend the ceilidh and drop in on your estranged daughter?" Ally didn't mean to sound sarcastic, but that was how it came out.

Maeve chewed her lip. "I… I've been thinking about you a lot, and I felt like I needed to see you. To be honest, I was worried, and I didn't know why."

Further in the cottage, the shower turned off and there was the rattle of a screen door opening. Ally had forgotten about Aiden. He would be out in a moment and come face to face with the mother she had not seen in twenty years. She told herself she didn't care. They were strangers, and she wasn't about to apologise for spending the night with Aiden. Besides, it wasn't as if her mother had a leg to stand on when it came to her personal life.

"There could be trouble," Ally said cautiously. "Maybe you shouldn't have come here." She wasn't sure what to say, how far to take this. Was Maeve like her? As far as she knew, her mother had not displayed any of the extrasensory abilities as Ally had.

Maeve's gaze suddenly fixed on Ally. "Your great-grandmother was a seer. A prophet. There were others in the family tree. We were known for it. I shouldn't have been surprised you were able to… see things, but I was. I was shocked, and frightened. The supernatural always made me uncomfortable. I stayed away from it. I think that might have been the reason I did not fight your father as hard as I should have when he refused to let you go. I told myself it was a battle I couldn't win, but that sounds more and more like a poor excuse every year."

Ally felt a stab of hurt. Her mother had found her too challenging and abandoned her. She should be angry, and yet… Ally understood. If she had a daughter who could talk to spirits and see past the veil, would she want to deal with her?

Well, of course she would, because Ally understood. But how could her mother, with such an aversion to the supernatural?

"There were a lot of drugs, a lot of women," Maeve continued. "Quentin… your father said he loved me, and I loved him, but I just couldn't cope. And then your… sight on top of that. I had to get away."

The door to the bathroom opened. Maeve stood up, looking nervous.

"Is there someone here with you? The woman at reception said you lived alone."

Ally wondered what else Mrs Shaw had shared. "I have a friend staying. Aiden," she said. "For the ceilidh." A 200-year-old English lord, she almost added, but then she'd have to explain things she doubted her mother would understand, even if she wanted to.

Maeve looked past Ally, and her eyes widened. Slowly she stood up.

Ally turned. Aiden was standing in the door-way. Thankfully, he was dressed, his hair wet and rumpled from the towel he held in his hands. He looked surprised to see someone new in the room, but his expression turned blank almost immediately.

"My apologies," he said. "I didn't realise you had a visitor."

"Aiden, this is my mother, Maeve MacDonald."

She saw the surprise in his dark eyes. "Your mother? I thought—"

"It's Maeve Arno now," Ally's mother smiled without any warmth. "And you're Aiden? You sound a little like Ally's father."

Ally preferred not to compare Aiden to her father. They were nothing alike.

"You came to Moyle to see Ally?" Aiden asked.

"Yes." Maeve's gaze turned to her daughter. "Well, one of the reasons. We were invited to the ceilidh by the owner of the island. It will be quite a collection of who's who."

Ally met Aiden's dark eyes and saw his concern. She was still looking at him when her mother added, "It was Mr Frazer I spoke to when I was deciding whether or not to come. He told me about you, Ally. It seems you have an admirer there," she added with a smile.

Ally watched Aiden's expression change from concern to unease. He glanced toward the door as if expecting some kind of ambush. Ally felt her muscles tighten. This was Stewart's doing, of course it was. He had brought Maeve here to the island, and he was directing proceedings just as he always did.

Maeve had sat down again, having no intention to leave just yet, and Ally found herself automatically making the tea, her mind chasing down all the possibilities as to why Stewart had involved Maeve in his grand plan. When her mother asked her questions about her life, she answered them, forcing herself to pay attention.

Maeve chatted about her life, too. She had no other children, had not wanted any, she added lightly, as if that did not sting Ally. She was comfortably off, and although her husband knew about her past, he didn't know the whole of it. She'd prefer he didn't, she added, with a look to Ally.

Eventually, they ran out of things to say and the silences grew longer between them. Maeve finished her tea and she stood up. "I'd better get back. Will you be at the hotel later?"

"Yes. I'll have to keep an eye on the shop. I'm not sure about the ceilidh…"

"Mr Frazer said it will be quite exclusive. Only his guests are attending. Are you invited?" She looked at Aiden.

"My friends and I are attending," he said, "and if I go, then so will Ally."

"Oh. May I ask how you and Alison met?" Maeve looked curiously from one to the other.

"We've known each other for years," Aiden said, and smiled at Ally.

It was true enough. They had known each other for over two hundred years if you wanted to be technical. Ally had been to the Hellfire Club in 1808 and Aiden was here in her time.

Maeve opened her mouth to ask more questions, then seemed to think better of it. She had no right to question a daughter she had abandoned, after all. The thought made Ally a little sad.

Ally saw her to the door and watched her go, feeling oddly relieved. She had thought about her mother for so long; at times she had desperately longed for her, but now she realised just how much the other women in the commune had stepped in and taken her place. Maeve wasn't a bad person, but she would never have understood Ally's abilities. She would probably have tried to stop them or send her to a head doctor to 'fix' her. Who knew what kind of long term damage her mother might have caused?

"He planned it," Aiden spoke behind her as she closed the door. "Stewart."

"Yes. Why, do you think?"

"He wants to cause as much chaos as he can," Aiden responded. "This gives you something else to worry about, to scatter your thoughts when you need to focus. He's a master manipulator, Ally. As you said, a spider in a web."

"And yet I think he did me a favour," she said softly.

He took her hands in his. "Because you can't see yourself living in a townhouse in Edinburgh, going to business lunches and being seen at the theatre?"

It was what her mother had talked about when she spoke of her comfortable life. Ally looked up at him with a smile. "Exactly. My God, we are so different, Aiden! I never realised. Do you think we just grew apart?"

"I think you are just different. You belong here, on Moyle, and she doesn't."

"Yet here she is," Ally mused. "I should tell her to go. Warn her."

"I'm not sure she'd listen to you. She prefers to think everything is as she sees it, no surface ripples, smooth sailing."

Ally gave him a hug, and felt comforted when he hugged her back. "Let's have lunch," she said. They'd missed out on breakfast. "Then we should get to the hotel. There's the shop to finish setting up, although I'm sure the women are already hard at it."

"And I need to talk to the others." Aiden bent to kiss her lips, but she could see he was distracted now, his thoughts on what was yet to come.

It was sobering to think that after tonight he might be gone. She didn't want to believe it, but she had to accept that it was a possibility. She knew she would miss him. Her heart may even break. At the very least, her life would never be the same again.

Chapter Twenty-Seven

A IDEN DIDN'T WANT to face the possibility that he may have no future. He and Ally had found a connection that was more than physical. He was falling in love with her. Aiden had never been in love before like this. He'd never allowed himself to fall in love, in part because he had learned early on that those he loved could easily be taken from him. But it was also true that he had never met anyone he was willing to risk such pain for.

Until now.

After lunch, Ally gathered the few remaining garments she needed to take to the hotel. She was a whirlwind of activity, and he would have liked to stay where he was, propping himself up against the doorjamb, watching her dart about as Wayward got under her feet. She was wearing tight jeans and a green patterned sweater, one of the Moyle ones, and her bright hair hung loose about her shoulders.

She was delicious.

She smiled over her shoulder. "Are you going to help?"

"What can I do?" But he didn't move and she laughed at him.

"Well, I guess I've done everything," she admitted. "We just have to get there now." With a wrinkle of her brow she looked out the window.

Aiden wondered if she was thinking about the blue man, Stewart, and whatever else they may encounter on their journey. He stood up to relieve her of her last armful of knitwear, and after a quick pat to Wayward, she led the way out of the door.

The air was still and cold, and although it wasn't raining, it felt as though it might. The sky had that steely grey look he was beginning to recognise as storm weather.

Ally smiled at him. "At least we have a cart this time. I don't think you enjoyed riding on my scooter."

He kissed the corner of her smiling mouth. "I didn't mind. There were many advantages to the scooter."

Such as holding her close and nuzzling against her hair. It wouldn't be the same in the cart.

"You seem stable now. I mean, you're not blinking on and off all the time. You wouldn't want to do that at the ceilidh."

"There are times when it would come in handy," he admitted. But if he was honest, he hadn't enjoyed being invisible. He knew it was a message from the Sorceress, a lesson, and he understood what she was trying to tell him. But he hadn't enjoyed no one being able to see or hear or touch him. Which was, of course, the point.

Once they were set, Ally started out along what was really only an earthen track. The golf cart bumped and shook and rattled alarmingly. Aiden couldn't hear the wash of the sea against the beach to his left, but he looked out in that direction and remembered the blue man. Was he out there in the cold waters of the Atlantic, watching them pass? The thought wasn't a particularly pleasant one, and he pushed it away. He'd have enough to worry about once they reached the hotel.

There had been one important piece of information that Ally's mother had shared with them. Stewart was already on Moyle. Maeve said 'Mr Frazer' had flown in early this morning but hadn't made his presence known yet. She wasn't sure exactly where he was, unfortunately, and had been confused as to why they were so eager to know.

Stewart was here, waiting for the moment when he would appear before them all and leave them gasping in awe at his cleverness.

His ego had to be the size of the moon.

Before long, Aiden saw the hotel ahead, its windows shining in the dull light. They found a place to park and a group of women gathered excitedly around the vehicle to help carry the wares inside.

Ally took a moment to introduce him, and there were curious glances and knowing grins. They thought he was her lover. Well, he was, wasn't he? There had been a few sly questions, but most of the women here were more interested in setting

up their shop on time, and wanted to get everything inside the hotel.

There was a great deal of chatter about the
ceilidh, and a great many complaints that they
had not been invited. From what Aiden could
understand, the usual ceilidh was like a country
dance, with music and dancing and no doubt a
lot of flirting between the men and women of
the island. He had attended something similar
when he was a boy. As he grew older, though not
wiser, he came to consider such entertainments
as unsophisticated.

In Grenada, the plantation workers sometimes
gathered in the hot, damp evenings to make their
own music, their voices rising and falling in the
clear air. Aiden had stayed inside with his father,
listening and drinking rum, wishing he was far
away. The guilt had eaten at him then. It still did.

But from what he could gather, this particular ceilidh was a far more sophisticated affair. It
was designed to be entertainment for the rich
and famous, and the knitting women whispered
that they had heard it was to be breathtakingly
spectacular, even for those who were bored and
thought they had seen everything.

"We plan on having a ceilidh of our own, in
Mrs MacKenzie's cottage," Mrs Morison said.
"Simple pleasures. Not this dolled up occasion
Mr Frazer organised for his posh friends."

"I'm glad," Ally said, and the look she gave
Aiden told him that she really was. Her friends
would be away from the hotel, and safe.

The hotel lobby seemed busier than before,

with new faces wearing expensive suits and pretty dresses. The heating meant no coats or scarves were necessary, but a gust of wind rattled the glass to remind them that if they wanted to go outside, they would need to rug up.

Aiden watched them organise and hoped Ally sold a lot of her knitted garments.

She glanced up as if she had heard his thoughts, and smiled. He nodded toward the elevators and she waved at him in understanding. He left her to it.

Upstairs in the suite, Loki leapt at him enthusiastically. Aiden held the big dog in his arms, laughing and rumpling his fur, before setting him down again. The others were gathered together and watched with amusement.

"He didn't miss you then?" Nicholas asked with a smirk.

"Or you him," Lorne added.

The remains of lunch were left on the table before them, as was the delicious smell of freshly brewed coffee. Aiden went to pour himself a cup.

"Where's Ally?" Linny asked. She'd tied her hair back and was wearing one of the Moyle sweaters over black jeans.

"Downstairs, helping set up the shop," he answered, then added, "Her mother is here. She said that Frazer... I mean Stewart invited her."

"I don't like the sound of that," Linny said.

"I think he's trying to affect her concentration. If she's worried about her mother, then she might not be able to focus on him."

Lorne was frowning. "I wonder if he sees her as

a threat? Is she really capable of saving the world?"

"Or destroying it," Maggie muttered. "That's what 'end of days' means, doesn't it? Maybe we should be scared of her too."

"Rubbish." Aiden felt his face heat up with emotion. "She only wants to help. Stewart knows how much she refused to buy into his bullshit about her being 'the one.' She came all the way to Moyle to get away from it."

Instead of taking offence, Maggie grinned at him. But before she could tease him, Aiden added, "Ally's mother also said that Stewart flew in early this morning."

Maggie's eyes widened. "He's here?"

"No doubt preparing for the grand entrance we talked about," Lorne said thoughtfully. "The moment is coming, my friends."

Aiden thought about telling them about the black mirror and Ally's scrying, but Mrs Noakes hadn't appeared as he'd hoped, and Essie was a personal matter. Maybe he would talk about it, but not right now.

Maggie was now on the phone to reception. "I believe Mr Frazer has arrived. Can you tell me which room he's in?" A pause. She tapped her foot impatiently. "Yes, the owner of the hotel… Mr Frazer, where is he?" She waited a little longer and then hung up.

"No luck?" Linny asked.

"They said he isn't staying in the hotel. They don't know where he is, and even if they did, they couldn't release that information."

"Maybe he's in a B&B," Linny said with a smirk.

"Porridge and smoked fish for breakfast; I can see him getting into that."

Maggie smiled despite herself, but she couldn't disguise her anxiety.

"Why has he invited these people, I wonder?" Lorne mused. "Oh, I know he wants to show off, make a spectacle of himself, but why these people? He hates us, and he did his best to wipe us from the earth. I would have thought his guests would also be the sort of people he would like to see ruined. Well-heeled, arrogant, privileged... surely they would be an anathema to Stewart?"

"Do you think he's setting a trap? Not just for us, but those he sees as the smug elite?" Linny leaned forward, vibrating with excitement. "That's it, isn't it? All these people he despises in the one place, with us. It has to be."

"How do we stop him?" Maggie's eyes were wide.

"We can't," Aiden said. "Not yet. We need him to attend the ceilidh so that we can put the binding ring on his finger and hand him over to the Sorceress. If we start warning people off, we'll lose him again."

The others agreed with him, albeit reluctantly.

"It'll be like lambs to the slaughter." Maggie reached for Lorne's hand.

"He might just want an audience," Lorne responded. "The sort of people that once looked down on him. He wants their regard, their esteem. He wants to see their envious amazement when he does whatever it is he is going to do."

They were silent for a moment. "There'll be a

demon involved." Nicholas sounded as if he had no doubt.

"There always is, isn't there? As long as it isn't our friend from Glasgow." Linny shuddered dramatically, but no one had the heart to laugh. They remembered the incubus that had made it impossible for Linny to sleep and had almost done terrible things to her. "Do you think he's going to try to send us all to the Dark World?" she added.

Nicholas shook his head. "Sigurd would be waiting for him. That one would like nothing more than to squash him under foot."

"The Sorceress seems to be about," Aiden spoke up. "She's been visiting me, and Ally saw her too. She insists that Ally is part of the team, and her presence here has meaning." He told them about the stopover at the crypt and watched the girls' eyes cloud with horror and the boys' faces fill with shame.

"So the witchy woman is orchestrating at least part of this," Linny said. "Why doesn't she just put an end to Stewart and be done with it?"

"It's not the way she works," Lorne drawled. "If it comes to an easy or difficult path, then she will always force us down the latter."

"It's her way of making us better, or so she would have us believe," Aiden said. "But you can't deny the results. You should have seen yourself when I went back. You were a right bastard."

Lorne looked uneasy, and gave a sideways glance at Maggie.

"He was," she agreed. "But not now. You're all lovely now."

There was some relieved laughter shared between them.

"One other thing," Aiden said, taking a deep breath. It was time to come clean about the scrying. "When we were at the cottage, Ally tried to summon the spirit of Mrs Noakes."

There was a gleam in Linny's eyes. "You're leading an exciting life these days, Aiden. Did it work?"

"No. She…" He shook his head. "No."

"Not a bad idea, however," Nicholas said thoughtfully. "I'm surprised her son hasn't done that himself. Surely he has the ability?"

"He knows she wouldn't approve." Lorne's smile was smug.

"That's what Ally said," Aiden said. "That's why we thought it might be a good idea."

Lorne considered that. "Yes," he said. "It would. I'd like nothing better than to see Mrs Noakes giving her son a good telling off."

They fell into silence, each of them letting that image play out in their minds.

"We should get some rest," Maggie said at last. "So that we can be sharp tonight."

For a moment, Aiden thought Lorne was going to remind them of how everything hung on their coming confrontation with Stewart, but they didn't really need to hear that again. They already knew that no matter what happened, Stewart would still surprise them. He had brought them all to Moyle, and there was nothing they could do but wait, and hope they could finally outwit him.

Chapter Twenty-Eight

ALLY COULDN'T HAVE been happier with how their pop-up had turned out. It was bright and interesting, and if the attention they were already getting was any indication, irresistible. The other women gathered around, flushed with excitement, and Ally prayed to whatever celestial beings were out there that everything would turn out all right tonight. That this fledgling business would grow and thrive, and they would all reap the rewards they deserved. And that there would be a world left where such things still mattered.

Mrs Morison had taken her aside earlier, telling her that Hamish was still a bit shaken after his adventure in the boglach. He didn't seem to know what had happened, but she blamed it on a late-night with his friends. It seemed Hamish had decided not to tell his aunt the truth, because the truth was unbelievable. Mrs Morison might be a Moyle woman, but she was also a stanch churchgoer. When the church had made its inroads into the Western Isles of Scotland, it had done its best to stamp out the local superstitions and myths.

Ally thought that was a shame. Such things were part of the islander way of life, part of their culture, but it wasn't up to her to tell the people that. She could imagine what they would think of her secret abilities. Best to keep all of that to herself.

Most of the shops were selling whiskey, but there was a tartan display from a group of weavers on another island, as well as sets of chess pieces carved from animal bone. Ally browsed until a nudge in her ribs and a nod from one of the women brought Aiden to her attention. He was watching her from across the room, and when she smiled at him, he took it as an invitation to join them.

"Ladies," he said, with a bow of his head. There were a few chuckles at that, and a few blushes. Aiden might portray himself as a modern man, but you didn't have to dig very far to find the Regency gentleman underneath.

"What do you think of our shop?" one of the women said proudly.

"Delightful," he replied, inspecting some of the garments on display. "I hope there will be something left for my friends."

"There's plenty for everyone," someone else assured him. "We're also taking orders if we don't have enough of what you want."

"Well, we're off to eat," Mrs Morison announced. "Coming?"

A woman who lived nearby had invited them to dine at her cottage. Then they would head off to their own ceilidh. A couple of them would

remain here to supervise any sales in the mean-
time.

"Aiden and his friends have asked me to stay,"
Ally explained.

Calls of "Enjoy yourself" carried them out of
the hotel, and Ally gave a sigh of relief. There was
only so much teasing she could stand at her age.
She wasn't a virgin schoolgirl, but her friends
sure made her feel like one at times. She couldn't
be cross though. They meant well, and they were
as fond of her as she was of them. They wanted
her to be happy, and they could obviously see
that she was around Aiden.

Aiden seemed anxious to get back to his friends,
and when they saw a queue at the elevator they
took the stairs instead. The ceilidh was to be in
the ballroom up on the next floor. The musicians
were already practising, the sound bright and
cheerful, but before they could get a look into
the large room, Mrs Shaw came rushing out and
almost ran into them.

"Oh!" Her eyes widened, then narrowed as she
saw Ally. "We're not starting for a couple of hours.
If you're looking for dinner, there is a restaurant
on the floor above," she snapped. "Though I
doubt there'll be room now, unless you booked."

"Thank you, but we're dining in the Marquis's
suite," Aiden said pleasantly.

Mrs Shaw almost huffed, but remembered her
manners in time and hurried off.

Ally smiled as Aiden took her hand. "That
showed her," she whispered.

Ally happened to glance into the ballroom

as they passed and saw her mother. Maeve was speaking to a man, their heads close together. Thinking it must be her mother's husband, Ally took a step toward them. Too late, she realised she recognised the man.

"Ari…" she breathed.

And, as if he sensed her gaze, Ari turned to face her. His mouth twitched into a half-smirk and his dark eyes blazed.

Ally felt a tingle run up her spine, the sort of thing that happened whenever something supernatural was afoot. A sense of foreboding, of expectation.

Something is coming.

In her head, she heard Ari's voice from all those years ago, telling her that she would bring on the end of days.

She hurried toward her mother, but before she reached her, Ari had turned and, impossibly, was gone. Just gone. He had stepped behind a passerby, but never reappeared on the other side. She reached Maeve, who looked startled, but forced a smile and began to make polite conversation.

"Who was that you were speaking to?" Ally said a little more forcefully than she'd intended.

Maeve frowned. "One of the waiters. Why? Alison, are you all right?"

"I thought…" Ally looked around and almost bumped into Aiden, who had come up behind her. "I'm sorry. I must have been mistaken."

But she hadn't been. She was sure she had seen Ari. Hadn't she…? She felt lost. Aiden took her hand, and she saw him exchange a questioning glance with her mother.

"Well, never mind," Maeve said bracingly. "I do hope to see you later at the festivities." With a nod to Aiden, she lost herself in the growing crowd.

Ally sighed. "You're going to think I'm crazy," she said, "but I thought I saw Ari."

Aiden bent his head to look into her face. "Not at all," he assured her. "Just now I thought I saw the Egyptian, the man who sold the runes to Lorne that brought forth the Destroyer."

Ally gasped. "You said you thought it might be the same man. But how could he be here?"

"It's Stewart," Aiden said. "They are one and the same. He does this all the time. He assumes someone else's identity to confuse and upset us. But it was him, you can be sure of it."

Ally felt a little better now. "Should we try to find him?"

"He'll be long gone, I'm afraid. He does that too. He's trying to unbalance you, provoke you, and you mustn't let him. We need you with us tonight, and we all must be completely focused. Come. Let's go upstairs to the others. They will want to hear this."

———◆———

Ally could see Aiden's news about Stewart brought everyone to a new level of alertness. This was the moment they had been waiting for, or dreading.

"So he's taken on the Egyptian's face, just as we thought," Lorne said. "Another for his menagerie.

We must be vigilant. He could be anywhere."

"Or anyone," Nicholas muttered. He fingered his scar. "He wanted you to see him," he nodded to Ally.

It was as Aiden had said, Stewart was trying to separate her from the others. There must be a reason for that. She was important. They needed her. The realisation made her all the more determined not to allow herself to be drawn in by Stewart's games.

"Aiden said you tried to contact Mrs Noakes last night," Maggie said. "Do you think you could try again? If anyone can shake his confidence, it's his mother, right?"

Ally hadn't planned on doing any scrying and her mirror was home at the cottage, but she could hardly refuse.

There was a mirrored door on the closet in the short hallway that led to the lounge. Aiden removed it with the help of Linny's nail file, and they set it up in a circle of furniture. With the blinds down and the lights extinguished, the room was almost completely dark. Ally sat cross-legged before the mirror. The reflections were distracting, despite the lack of light, but she did her best to ignore the shifting shapes and shadows.

"Perhaps if you call for her," she said, looking to Lorne. She could not see more than his silhouette right now.

A moment later, Lorne spoke in a low voice. "Mrs Noakes. Will you come to us? Will you help us? Your son is determined to destroy the world and us with it, and you need to… you need to…"

"Give him a good hard slap?" Linny suggested and was quickly hushed.

"He will listen to you," Lorne went on after a pause. "He wants your love and your approval, and he will listen if you tell him to stop. Will you come to us? Will you help us? Will you help me?"

The silence was profound. Ally stared into the void, hoping that Mrs Noakes would suddenly appear. A mist seemed to form over the glass, thickening, until she felt as if she could put her hand through it and, instead of touching that cold surface, she would in fact find nothingness. Slowly she stretched out, her fingers disappearing into the vapour moving over the mirror. She focused on the thought of Mrs Noakes, and when first her wrist and then her lower arm, and finally her elbow vanished into the mist, she heard the gasps behind her.

It briefly shook her out of her focus, but she forced away any distraction. The mirror had gone and there was nothing behind the mist, only empty space, but it wasn't unoccupied because she could feel a presence on the other side creeping closer.

"Mrs Noakes?" Lorne spoke again, and to Ally his voice was suddenly that of a small child. "I need you," he said. "Without you, I doubt I would have survived my grandmother's cruelty after my mother died. You were my only friend."

Suddenly, something beyond the mist brushed her fingers... and gripped. Another hand. Cold as ice.

It shocked Ally so much that she wrenched her

arm back, forcing whatever held her to let go, and then lost her balance as she fell backwards onto the carpet. Before her, the white fog was alive with movement, swirling and pulsating, and then abruptly it was sucked back, deep into the mirror.

The room erupted. Ally felt Aiden's warm hands—so different from that icy one—helping her up. "Are you all right? Ally?"

"Yes. Yes I am." She took a breath. She felt shaky. "I'm sorry. I thought for a moment she was there, but…"

The rest of the group were just as shaken as her, and disappointed too. Ally tried not to feel a failure, but it wasn't easy.

"Should we skip dinner?" Linny said.

"No." Lorne glanced at Maggie. "We should eat. We need to be as strong as we can possibly be."

Lorne rang up the restaurant, and a meal was delivered. It was perfect, a showcase for the local fishing industry, accompanied by various Scottish delicacies. At any other time, Ally would have applauded the hotel's efforts. But right now she could barely swallow a mouthful. The others seemed to be having the same difficulty. The silence grew as everyone mulled their own thoughts and what was still to come.

Outside, the lights from the hotel fell across the jetty and the bay. The sounds of music drifted up from the ballroom, and laughter came from the street as more guests arrived at the building, ready to enjoy themselves. There had been a helicopter ferrying them in from the mainland for hours.

All too soon it was time to go to the ceilidh. Ally had brought a change of clothes, a pair of black pants and a longer tartan tunic in the Mac-Donald colours. The other women also changed, Maggie into a white dress with a tartan silk scarf and Linny in jeans and a short-sleeved sweater in what she said were loosely McNab colours. "Whatever they are."

The three men were elegant as always in black, casual wear. They wouldn't be out of place in the crowd tonight, and could fit in with the rest while keeping a close eye on proceedings.

"Are we ready?" Lorne asked as they gathered at the door.

"Aye," Nicholas and Aiden replied loudly.

"Then let us go forth, my friends. Let Stewart review whatever surprise he has for us, because it will be his last. Tonight, we make things right."

It was as good a motivational speech as any, Ally thought, as she started after them toward the stairs. Aiden took her hand, squeezing her fingers, and she squeezed them back. Whatever happened in the next couple of hours, they would face it together.

Chapter Twenty-Nine

HOOUK GAZED UP at the tall, brightly lit building. The storm had passed and his blue skin camouflaged him well in the still waters by the jetty. He preferred not to come where the dry ones were, but tonight he felt he had no choice. The woman with hair like a sunset had saved his life, and he knew she was in danger. The magic his people were known for told him so, and he had come to warn her of the calamity that was approaching.

His people came from a time when magic flowed like rivers, and creatures that lived within the magic came in every shape and size. Until the dry ones made it their domain alone. In olden days the blue men were hunted, so they took their revenge, sinking ships and drowning sailors. For the watery places belonged to them.

No longer. Times had changed and now Hoouk's people were just legends. There was no place in this world for his kind anymore, and all except him had moved on in one way of another. Only Hoouk remained—he had loved the oceans too much to leave them.

He had lived a vast amount of time already, through centuries of change, but he was afraid that what would happen tonight would eclipse all of them. Well, he was old, his life probably nearly at an end anyway. And she had saved his life when most would have turned away or killed him quickly.

They had a connection, him and her. Something tied them together. Her kindness in saving him as he lay tangled in the nets, a creature so different from herself, deserved an act of equal generosity. Even if it was his last.

Again he looked up at the tall structure. He would wait until the moment was right and then he would slip inside. Turning back to the bay, Hoouk lowered himself into the water and sank beneath the surface.

Chapter Thirty

THEY DESCENDED THE stairs instead of taking the lift and then split up. As Ally approached the ballroom, where the ceilidh was taking place, she began to feel a tingle. She had felt it earlier, before she saw Ari/Stewart with her mother. Something was in the air, watching and waiting. But as she got closer to her destination, the sense of foreboding had grown darker and heavier. She was starting to feel sick.

This was not good.

She looked at the others, but none of them seemed to be sharing the same feelings, and she decided not to say anything. Best not to make them any more anxious.

Mrs Shaw was still rushing about, done up in a tartan skirt and a colourful sash over her white blouse. Her cheeks were flushed, but she still had time to give Ally a dirty look while sending a flirty one to Aiden.

"There's no charge tonight," she said. "Mr Frazer wants everyone to enjoy themselves. He's a very generous man. There must be five hundred people here!"

Aiden and Ally exchanged a look, and once they were away from Mrs Shaw's listening ears, they stopped to talk.

"Generous? My guess is he wants as many people here as possible for whatever he has planned," Aiden said soberly.

Ally agreed. The feeling of nausea was getting worse, but she did her best to ignore it. She peered into the crowd, trying to see what might be causing her reaction, but everyone seemed to be enjoying themselves. The music was loud and jaunty. Voices rose and fell, interspersed with laughter. She recognised quite a few famous faces—a politician and an actor, a singer and a television host.

"What is it?" Aiden asked. He was more tuned into her than she had realised, his dark eyes full of questions.

"I don't know. I can feel something. As if…" She shook her head, searching for words that wouldn't come. Across the room, Lorne and Maggie stood close together, watching the crowd. Another scan of the room showed Linny and Nicholas trying to fit in with the other dancers. Nicholas couldn't exactly manage a jig with his lame leg, but they were swaying together, Linny's head resting on his shoulder. Her fair hair was bright against the dark cloth.

"As if what?" Aiden repeated, his eyes still on her. "What do you feel?"

"It's similar to the feeling I get when there's a spirit nearby, deciding whether or not to make contact… But at the same time it's different. And much, much stronger. Like a wave rushing toward me and I can't get out of the way."

This is not good. The words had become a mantra in her head, throbbing in the background like a drum, or a headache.

Aiden took her hand and looked around, catching sight of Lorne, and then moved in that direction.

Maggie was wearing a white cockade in her hair and smiled as they approached. "I thought I should get into the spirit and celebrate the Scottish thing," she said. "I'm sure my ancestors were Jacobites. They wouldn't have towed the government line." Her cheeks were flushed and there was a sparkle in her eyes. The light of battle, Ally thought. Maggie was going to war.

"I feel something," Ally said quietly. "I think Stewart is opening a door between this world and the other world. He's bringing something through, something that shouldn't be here."

"Something." Lorne said quietly.

"What can we do?" Maggie placed a hand over the swell of her belly.

"He'll be arrogant, thinking he's unstoppable," Aiden reminded them. "He'll be full of his own importance. You know what he's like. Before, we didn't really know what he was capable of, we didn't really know him. Now we do."

Lorne's icy blue eyes lit up. "Yes. We know him. He has his audience now, and if I choose the right moment, I can get the ring on his finger. We can end this, my friends. I only need the opportunity."

"We could create a distraction," Maggie said.

Lorne looked at her to argue, only to change his mind. They had obviously already had this matter out once this evening.

"I know this is about all of us, but at the heart of it is Stewart's hatred for you," Maggie said. "It's his only true blind spot. And because of your feelings for me, I'm the perfect distraction. He'll want to use me to get to you. If playing into that is what it takes to save us, then I will."

Ally could see the conflicting feelings in the Marquis's face, but he nodded, reluctantly, conceding the point, "But remember, my love, if I lose you, then it is all over for me."

She went into his arms, murmuring something too low to hear, and Ally looked away, allowing them their intimate moment.

Just then, there was a crackle of sound from the dais as someone came onto the microphone.

"What a wonderful turn out tonight!" Ally recognised the voice of the new hotel manager. "Mr Frazer has been very generous and I know you'll all want to show your appreciation tonight. He's putting Moyle on the map as an elite resort destination. This is just the start. He tells me that tonight will be a night none of us will ever forget!"

There were some cheers but more of the crowd exchanged glances and raised eyebrows. Was it because they felt they had already seen everything there was to see, that their wealth and power gave them that privilege? Or were they unimpressed with Mr Frazer?

The response had been a little too half-hearted for the manager's liking. He geed them up into another round of applause before continuing. "Mr Frazer will be here soon. I'll let him tell you what he has in store—it's been rather hush-hush. But for now, enjoy yourselves!"

He added a few words in careful Gaelic—he'd obviously been practicing. Linny snorted in derision and muttered something about 'outlanders'—and then the music started up again. With a whoop, some professional dancers appeared from behind a curtained doorway. They circled the room, laughing and turning to the tune of fiddle and flute, kilts and skirts swinging.

"Should we dance?" Aiden asked, nodding toward where Nicholas and Linny had again taken to the floor.

"Why not?" Ally said. "We might not get another chance."

Aiden drew her into the crowd. Ally hadn't expected to dance tonight, but as they joined the others, she found there was nothing she wanted more than to dance with Aiden. His hand was strong and warm as he swung her about. He circled her around and then back into his arms, and when she looked up, she saw that lustful gleam in his eyes. He was thinking about their lovemaking earlier.

Her heart swelled, and for a time she forgot about her fears for the future, about what might happen. The sensation was still there, the sick feeling, the headache throbbing like an infected wound, but she was able to push it to the background as she gave herself this moment with Aiden.

And then, abruptly, the music came to a discordant halt.

Ally and Aiden stopped to see what was going on, with an equally puzzled crowd. People were looking toward the door that led into the ballroom.

As a gap opened before her, Ally noticed a group of people, and once again saw the hotel manager. Beside him was a slight man with glasses. It was Stewart, the same man she had seen at the Hellfire Club. Now murmurs punctuated the hush as everyone waited for what would come next. There were a few sniggers at the very idea that there was anything mind-boggling enough here to impress them.

"Ladies and gentleman, or lassies and lads," the manager said in that self-conscious way that garnered a chuckle or two. "I have the privilege of introducing the venerable Mr Frazer, the owner of Moyle, who is with us tonight to share in our celebrations. Those of you who knew and loved the late Professor Simon Frazer… Well, I'm sure you will extend a warm welcome to his cousin, Mr Stewart Frazer."

There was some clapping, which then grew louder. But before 'Frazer' had a chance to speak, a voice rose from the back of the room and grew louder as the person moved forward.

Maggie.

"You are not Simon's cousin! You liar. You thief. The man was my husband! How dare you steal everything from him? You monster!"

Now there were startled gasps and outcries of 'Shame!' 'Be quiet, madam!' Ally wanted to go to Maggie, but her gaze was fixed on Stewart, still standing beside the manager. He smiled as if nothing was wrong, or maybe he was smiling because everything was going exactly as he wanted it to.

"He's loving this," Aiden breathed against her ear. "He must have expected it."

Maggie was still castigating him, but Lorne had caught up with her now, holding her against him, while he glared at Stewart at the same time. And still the man smiled, his glasses reflecting the light, clearly enjoying this moment.

This was it. The grand finale. A new wave of sickness washed over Ally. At the same time, her head spun, as invisible forces pushed forward through the veil between the worlds, breaking through.

And with a sense of dread, she knew no one could stop it.

Chapter Thirty-One

SOMEONE SCREAMED, THE sound shrill and full of terror.

Aiden felt the shock of it undulate through the room, a swell that grew and grew as more people joined the cacophony. He turned his head, trying to see what the cause of the hysteria was, and noticed that some people in the crowd no longer looked quite right. He blinked and looked again.

At first, he thought they were in costume. But costumes such as these were beyond the ability of any human being to create. As if seeking answers, his gaze went to Stewart, and his blood froze.

The Destroyer. The very demon that had started all of this was there in the doorway right behind Stewart. Those yellow fangs and the long white hair, with only an animal skin to cover its nakedness. Aiden's head jerked towards Lorne, and he found his friend also staring at the foul creature, his shoulders stiff and his face a rictus of horror.

Lorne pulled Maggie behind him and moved closer to Aiden and Ally. Aiden looked around desperately for Nicholas and Linny but could no longer see them.

Now something else caught his eye. The blue man. He was so close that he must have walked right up to them without anyone noticing, yet here he was. Those strange eyes were fixed on Ally.

"Ally," Aiden croaked.

"What?" She turned her head and saw him. For a moment they stared at each other, and Aiden felt her hand go slack in his. He gripped tighter.

The creature made a strange hissing sound that passed for words. Ally seemed to understand it, or perhaps she was communicating telepathically. "He says there is great danger," she said. "We should go while we can."

"We can't go," Aiden said hollowly, turning about as someone else gave a hysterical laugh. Did these people think it was a joke? Part of the show?

Ally leaned in toward the blue man. "Thank you," she told him, and it sounded heartfelt. "I can't go, but you should. Find somewhere safe."

The storm kelpie reached out and brushed his clawed fingers over hers, and for a brief moment he and Ally clasped hands.

But Aiden had no time for niceties. He pulled her away from the creature, which vanished into the crowd. Then, to his relief, Nicholas was suddenly by his side, breathing hard, with Linny wide-eyed beside him.

"Zany is here," his friend growled.

Just then, a small man popped out of the now panicked crowd and turned a cartwheel. He gave them a wink before he zigzagged away, avoiding people's legs with ease.

There were even more creatures now. Everywhere he looked, Aiden could see demons and monsters roaming the room. Each one seemed to slip into view without ever revealing how they had entered. And their numbers continued to grow.

The door between the mortal world and the Dark World was wide open and the horrors it had contained were pushing through. Yet the fear first expressed by the crowd seemed to have dissipated. The people didn't realise what danger they were in, and most expressed admiration for such magnificent costumes. Some were even taking selfies with what appeared to be a pot-bellied pig demon with tusks.

A voice called out. "Alison!" Aiden swung around. Stewart had hold of Maeve and Ally's mother looked panicked.

But Stewart was focussed on Ally, as if he was sending her a warning against interfering. Next thing, Maeve gave her captor a kick in the shins and scuttled away to safety.

Ally took a step, shook her head as if to clear it, and took another. Her legs gave way.

Aiden grabbed hold of her, but before he could ask what was wrong Stewart cried out a word that sounded rather like some of those Lorne had chanted when he brought the Destroyer into the mortal world.

There was a moment of complete silence, and then the creatures attacked.

He saw the Destroyer launched itself at a man,

taking him down to the ground, and the other creatures followed suit. Panic broke out anew when everyone realised the danger they were in and tried to flee, only to find the doors to every exit locked. As one man shook and rattled at them, he was taken down by a demon with horns and a forked tail. Blood sprayed in an arc and the people who had come to help turned about and ran.

Aiden felt his gorge rise, but he pushed it aside. No time for that. "We have to get to Stewart," he shouted above the chaos. "Only we can stop this."

He slipped his arms around Ally, taking most of her weight, and looked over the heads of those around him, doing his best to ignore the carnage. Stewart was standing on the dais now—the musicians had long since fled their posts—his mouth stretched wide with a grin of pure enjoyment. The ballroom was becoming a house of slaughter. This was always his intent, to sacrifice those who had despised him in his previous life. Revenge, brutal and final. And by the expression on Stewart's face, it was sweet indeed.

"Come on." Aiden began to move, but Ally had become a dead weight. He paused to swing her up into his arms before jogging toward Stewart. The others hurried to catch up, avoiding the demons as best they could. The Destroyer had finished with its victim and now meant to go after them, but Zany came out of nowhere, rolled between its legs, and sent it tumbling to the ground.

"Oopsie!" the little man sniggered.

"Jesus, did you see that?" Linny demanded.

"Whose side is he on?"

"Ours, I think," Nicholas muttered. "For now."

Stewart watched a particularly nasty scene between a werewolf demon and a human hiding with others under the buffet table, but now his gaze turned as they approached.

"Ah," he said, giving his little cough. "There you all are. Enjoying yourselves? Plenty more to come." He rubbed his hands together in glee, the malevolence in his face quite startling. He looked back at the carnage. "Hiding under a buffet table. How appropriate."

"You bastard," Maggie's voice broke with pain and rage. There was a splatter of blood across her dress, but it wasn't hers. All about them, people were being torn to pieces. "You deserve to suffer. I hope you do. I hope... I hope..."

"How sad. Still blinded by your love for the Marquis, I see." He sighed with fake regret. "I had hoped you might have seen the light by now, Maggie. And look, there is dear Linny and her limping Earl. Another sad case. And Aiden," he said with a bright smile as if they were all friends. "Did you enjoy your journey into the past? The Hellfire Club, what a waste of space. Did that stupid witch expect you to change the course of history? We all know Lorne never listens to anyone."

"I'm listening to you," Lorne said in a hard voice. "Your foul words pollute the very air we breathe. Others move beyond life's disappointments, yet you are not capable of feeling anything but hate."

Stewart's mouth hardened, then he was smiling again. "You're mistaken, Marquis. I am not the villain here. I never have been. It's you. You, much like everyone in this room, represent everything that is wrong. Corrupt and decadent, you call yourselves the elite? You must be punished, and I intend to see it happen."

There was a terrible shriek as a winged creature darted over them. It was pursuing a woman in a sparkly dress, but as it passed by Aiden holding Ally, it veered away with another shriek. One of its clawed feet caught in Linny's long hair. She cried out, struggling to free herself, and Nicholas grabbed the creature's leg and struck at it with his cane. It released her and fled, and Linny crumpled against him, quaking in rage and fear.

"Oh dear." Stewart's face was screwed up with false concern. "That was close. It would be a shame if you were silenced forever, Linny."

"She's worth a million of you, you monster," Nicholas growled.

Stewart laughed, genuinely amused. Then, just as abruptly, his expression shifted into malice. "You morons, did you really think you'd still be standing here, alive, if I did not wish it? I wanted you here tonight so that you could see what I have become. Risen from a snivelling bastard to the supreme master of all before him! And what are you, Marquis? Still the selfish, stupid, worthless fellow you always were."

Stewart's rant gave Aiden a chance to check on Ally. She seemed to be unconscious, yet her eyes were open. He leaned in and felt the caress of her warm breath on his face.

"Ally?" he whispered, and gave her a little shake. "Are you okay?"

She murmured something, her words slurring as if she was drunk. "Dark," he thought she said. "On and on... Trying to find my way... Lost... Aiden, help me..."

"I'm here." He held her closer and brushed his lips against her temple. Nicholas nudged him, hard, and Aiden growled, then turned to see what his friend was looking at. Stewart was still carrying on, but a flash of movement behind him caught Aiden's eye.

Zany and the blue man were creeping across the dais toward the self-proclaimed supreme master. Nicholas grabbed Lorne's arm, but their friend had already seen the unlikely duo. Stewart must have noted their interaction because he broke off his speech and began to turn, just as Zany caught hold of his legs and tipped him over. For all his powers, Stewart fell like a sack of flour, and the blue man flung himself across Stewart's middle, pinning him down. Lorne launched onto the dais, tearing the ring from the chain about his neck, and grabbing Stewart's wrist.

Nearby, the flying monster had caught its prey and flew past with the woman in the sparkly dress screaming in its beak. Another demon was tearing at a man in a thousand dollar suit, while something slimy and evil removed a well-known actor's head.

Aiden tuned out the chaos playing out all around them and set Ally down, resting her back against the dais. Maggie and Linny shuffled to her side to protect her. He straightened just in time to see the Destroyer lift the blue man from its master and fling him across the room. As the creature turned to deal with Lorne, Nicholas struck it around the head with his walking stick. The Destroyer fell and did not get up.

Aiden rushed to help Lorne in the fight, pinning down Stewart's thrashing legs. Finally he forced Stewart's clenched fist open and jammed the Sorceress's ring onto his finger.

"There!" Lorne cried out. "Got you, you cad!"

They had done it! Linny gave a squeal of joy, and Nicholas gave a sharp laugh of disbelief. Tears were running down Maggie's cheeks as Lorne turned to her, his blue eyes full of wonder.

"We did it!" Aiden looked to Ally to share his joy, but she wasn't looking at him, or any of them. Her head was bowed to her chest, her auburn hair strewn over her face. Something is wrong. Very wrong. She had told him she was feeling unwell, that there was something coming…

Stewart clapped his hands together. A slow, ironic clap.

"Oh well done," he mocked as he picked himself up from the ground. "Did you really think your stupid ring would do anything? I've seen more impressive rings inside cereal boxes."

Now Stewart dropped to his knees before them, but there was no doubt who was the master here. "Did you really think it would be this easy?" he said. "It was all part of the game. Don't you see? I won the moment you all entered this room."

The power emanating from him grew even stronger now. Aiden felt himself begin to tremble. Ally finally lifted her head, but she was not looking at him. Her gaze was turned inward, and her green eyes were ablaze, red fire flickering in their depths, and her face had become as white as a corpse.

She sprang to her feet as if gravity held no sway over her. As if her energy was boundless.

"Ally!"

The others could see it too—Ally was no longer Ally.

"What have you done to her?" Maggie cried out.

"Me?" Stewart said, "I have done nothing. The power was always there, inside her, but suppressed. Opening the door to the Dark World has brought it forth, and made it a thousand times stronger. You see?"

As he spoke, one of the demons trotted toward them on cloven hooves, but on seeing Ally, turned and ran the other way.

"You see?" Stewart repeated with glee. "They recognise her power. They fear who she really is."

"No," Aiden said, "it's Ally. She's not... She isn't..."

Stewart ignored him. "She is doing just as was prophesied, as I prophesied. Only once in a millennia does someone like your Ally come along. She is the one, and the world is about to end, and when it does, she and I will be the rulers of all mortals. We will reign over the between-world and cast that stupid witch out. The Dark World will fall, and Sigurd will beg me to spare him. I won't. And then there is the Underworld." He smiled with malevolence. "That is where you will go, my dear Lorne. You and your friends, for all eternity!"

Aiden wanted to launch himself at Stewart, tear him limb from limb, but he could not keep his gaze from Ally. Only she was no longer Ally. He had fallen in love and that love was lost, and it felt as if all his striving, all his determination to change, was for nothing.

"Ally?" he called out, but she was blind to him. Energy crackled around her, and the flames in her eyes danced higher as she looked about her. She smiled, and it froze the blood in his veins.

Stewart gave them his fake sympathetic smile. "Oh, is your heart broken, Aiden? You pitiful little man, she is mine, just as she always was. This is our time." Then in a commanding voice that seemed to echo around them, "Ally, come to me!"

Aiden could only watch in horror as Ally went obediently to Stewart's side, leaping up onto the dais. She floated above the floor before she settled. "Kill them," she cried, looking about her with those strange, flame-ridden eyes. "Kill them all!"

Those rich guests who were still alive had barricaded themselves in a corner, overturning tables and holding the creatures back with chairs. The demons surrounding them were playing with them, feeding off their fear, but it wouldn't be long before they swatted the defences aside and finished what they had started.

Aiden knew it was Stewart's will alone protecting him and his friends, but that would not
last. He wondered how much longer they would
survive. The power that had been released was
surging all around them. There was a hard thrum-
ming sound, growing stronger and stronger.

Ally was gone, the familiar shell of her was
inhabited by the lust for all-consuming power.
And yet... surely a part of her remained? It had
to. Ally was strong. She had walked away from
Stewart before when he was pretending to be
Ari. Aiden could not, did not accept she could be
so easily lost.

A wail rose up from the throats of humans and
demons alike. A dark vortex was forming above
them, a tornado of onyx with silver flashes. It
swirled and grew wider, swallowing up the chan-
deliers, until it stretched from one side of the
ballroom to the other. Then it began to creep
down the walls.

"A portal!" Nicholas shouted. There was a gale
blowing now, and his dark hair was whipping
around his face.

"The door," Stewart roared his satisfaction.
"The door to the Underworld opens. Prepare for
the end."

Stewart's face was ablaze, his glasses reflecting
the horrors about him. "Yes!" he shouted. "It
begins! Yes!"

Aiden closed his eyes. The ring hadn't worked.
The Sorceress was nowhere to be seen. This really
was the end then. His second chance at life was
all for naught, and God knew where they would

all end up. He looked again toward Ally, who now stood beside Stewart. A ball of lightning sprang out of the portal and there was a stench of burning flesh, followed by another. Ironically it was mostly the demons who were being incinerated, while the humans were safe behind their barricade. Aiden turned to his friends one last time.

Lorne and Maggie stood holding each other tight, Nicholas and Linny were also in each other's arms. Aiden was more than ever aware that he stood alone. His mind turned to Loki, his faithful hound, who had been with him through so much. He hoped Loki was safe still, that somehow he would survive once Aiden was gone.

Something clasped his ankle. He jumped back, thinking of the creatures he had seen tonight, but he saw through the smoke the shimmer of blue. Something made him kneel down, and there was the blue man, still alive but mortally injured. Those strange eyes met his. The creature was trying to tell him something, not with words, but telepathically. Something in the being's expression made him trust him... He let his mind open and suddenly it was full of images.

For a moment he thought it was simply the final regrets of a creature who had spent his life in the ocean, but then there was an image of Ally gazing down, her face full of compassion... It was Ally on the beach when she set the blue man free. As Aiden stared into those outlandish eyes, he began to see more images of Ally. But this time, she was somewhere dark. A tunnel with dripping walls, dark and endless. He remembered what Ally had said to him, before Stewart took her over: On and on. Lost.

The place he was seeing in his mind was familiar, so very familiar. The between-worlds!

But how could that be? Ally was here with Stewart. Aiden lifted his head and stared at Ally, and as if the pieces clicked together in his head, he saw everything with fresh eyes. The way she floated above the floor, the way her hair flickered about her like the gorgon's serpents, and the faint blue light that had begun to shine from her chalk-white face.

"That isn't Ally," he said, but he wasn't sure anyone could hear him over the clamour. "Ally isn't here."

Just then, Aiden's nose and eyes stung. There was a pungent smell in the air. Linny covered her hands over her face, while Nicholas held his arm over his. He dropped it long enough to say, "Brimstone!" in a desolate voice.

Stewart roared and lifted his arms, like a conductor about to bring the orchestra to a crashing finale. At least Ally was safe, Aiden thought. He met the blue man's eyes one last time before they closed forever, thanking him. Because whatever happened now, Ally was safe in the between-worlds, and Aiden could bear just about anything as long as the woman he loved was safe.

It happened so quickly. Ally fell forward, tumbling off the edge of the dais, but it seemed as if her body had split in two, because as Aiden rushed to catch her he could see another Ally still standing by Stewart.

She fell into his arms, gasping and whimpering, and as he clasped her close, he could feel her tremble. She lifted her head and Ally's green eyes gazed up at him in question.

"You were in the between-worlds," he said. "The blue man showed me."

Before she could answer, there was a tearing sound, as if something huge had been rent in two. A manic grin took over Lorne's soot covered face. Aiden followed his gaze. Someone stood behind Stewart. An old woman in an old-fashioned gown, her grey hair covered in a cap, her back a little stooped. She should have been out of place in this house of horrors, but as she moved forward, she seemed to know exactly what she was doing.

It was Mrs Noakes.

"Boy!" she called, her crackly voice raised above the tumult.

Stewart froze. The gleeful victory washed from his face, taking all the colour with it until he was a sickly shade of green. Very slowly he turned around. "Mother?" His voice wavered with uncertainty.

Ally's face blanked in shock. "I know her! She was beside the bed, Aiden. After the scrying and Essie… She was peering down at us. And that voice! I recognise it. She came to me once, long ago, to warn me." Tears filled her eyes. "Oh God, all along it was Mrs Noakes."

"You wicked boy," the woman scolded, circling him while the Ally doppelganger kept out of the way. "What have you done now?"

"I-I haven't," he stammered, wildly different from his master of the universe facade. "It wasn't my fault. What are you doing here, Mother?"

"Did you think I wasn't watching you? You are my son. I wanted to see what you had made of your life. The choices you made. And I am very disappointed."

"Disappointed?" Stewart snapped out of his shock and snarled. "I am making things right. I have learned to control the universe. I am more powerful than any other creature. Living things cringe with fear when I pass. And you are disappointed?"

The old woman went on as if he hadn't spoken. "Do you wonder why I never held you in my arms?" She leaned in close, right into his face. "Why I never loved you as a son should be loved?"

"I know why! You loved Lorne best!" Stewart shouted.

Mrs Noakes poked him in the chest. "And that excuses your behaviour? Lorne's grandmother hated him. His life was a misery, and yet he still managed to be kind. Did you not wonder where our fresh loaves of bread came from? The cook would never have bothered to send them to us. Or the box of apples from the orchard? What of the warm blankets for our beds? That was all Lorne. He takes care of those he loves. While you..." and she poked him again. "All you wanted to do was whine and complain, to blame, and when something fell into your power that was weak you killed it. I know. I buried the poor cat. You always were evil, boy. Nothing has changed."

"If you had only shown me one tiny fraction of the affection you gave to him!" and Stewart turned and pointed at Lorne. "All I wanted was some sign that you loved me, your son."

"When you were born, I loved you, but before long I saw the way you were. Something was awry with you, and I could not fix it. All I could do was try to keep you away from those you might harm. I hoped you might change, but you only got worse as the years passed. There is nothing to be done but send you down to the Underworld where you can find others like yourself, kept in a place you can do no harm."

"No! I am too close! I want to show you what—"

"It is too late. She is already here for you."

"She…?"

"Thank you, Mrs Noakes." The voice echoed about them and a blue light shone across their faces. The Sorceress stepped out of her disguise. The form of Ally shimmered and vanished, while the real Ally still clung to Aiden.

Stewart turned, suddenly realizing that the Sorceress had tricked him and his mother had betrayed him. He looked furious and yet hurt beyond bearing. "Nooo!" he shouted, like a pet-ulant boy. "What have you done, Mother?"

Mrs Noakes folded her hands at her waist. "It is for your own good."

"You foul bitch!" Stewart roared.

Mrs Noakes smiled with satisfaction. "Ah, there he is. There's my son."

"What have you done to Ally?" Stewart turned to the Sorceress, almost sobbing in his rage. "All these years I have planned to use her powers. All these years I have schemed for this moment."

"You planned and schemed?" she replied. "I have had your measure from the very beginning. Ally isn't the one, you fool. She never was. I only made you think it was so, and you fell into my trap." The Sorceress drifted closer. "Now come with me. I have a place for wicked boys."

Stewart cried out, but he was already shrinking before their eyes. And now the humming noise reached a screaming crescendo. A moment later, he was gone. The dark clouds of the portal rumbled and turned a few more times, sucking the demons into its maw, and then began to dissipate.

Mrs Noakes lingered a moment longer before she began to fade as well. Her gaze turned to Lorne, and she smiled. "Charles," was all she said.

"Thank you," he whispered, but she was already gone.

The room became silent. People in the room had begun to stir, those who were still alive, but they kept their distance like frightened animals.

"You have done well, my Hellfire boys." The Sorceress looked extremely pleased with herself. "The threat of Stewart has been removed. He is crushed and he will not rise again."

"What about the ring?" Lorne said, sounding hoarse from the atmospheric effects. "We did as you said and put it on his finger and he laughed."

"The important thing is you did as I said."

Maggie gave a shaky laugh. "It was never going

to work, was it? You had us running around in circles and it was never going to work!"

"It gave you focus," the witch answered sternly.

Just then, a huge man with blond hair appeared at the Sorceress's side, dressed in a tuxedo like he had been late for the party.

"Sigurd," Nicholas said. It seemed he was not looking forward to this reunion.

"We are all here, are we?" Sigurd boomed. "It is done." He looked to the Sorceress, towering over her, and a smile twitched his lips.

"It is," she said coyly. "We should join forces more often, Sigurd. Who knows what great deeds we could accomplish?"

"I'd rather not have the occasion to," he responded. "Let peace reign in all the worlds."

"Did you see me?" It was Zany, skipping about.

"Indeed we did," the Sorceress said dryly. "You served your purpose. Now begone."

The little man vanished in a puff of smoke.

"Where is Hoouk?" the Sorceress demanded. She gestured and the blue man appeared before her, made whole again. "You are brave and we thank you," she told him. "I am sending you to your people, in the world where they now reside."

His smile brought tears to Ally's eyes.

They could hear someone calling Ally's name, and the door to a storage cabinet near the drinks table began to open. It looked too small to hold much, but Maeve and her husband were crawling out of it, alive but shaken. As they stood up, a rumpled Mrs Shaw with torn clothing followed, before she slumped against the wall and slid slowly down in exhaustion. Ally went to hug her mother, their reunion far warmer than the one earlier in the day.

Aiden sighed and stood with the other men. It was over, but that meant that this was their moment of reckoning.

The Sorceress grew silent, her gaze serious, and Aiden's heart sank. Whatever she was about to say would not be good. He tried to prepare himself, but his heart was stuck in his throat.

"The past is already written," she said. Was that a trace of regret in her voice? "You must go back. The mob will deal with you. But do not despair. You have escaped Stewart's fate. I am proud of my Hellfire boys."

"At least let us say goodbye—" Lorne began desperately.

"We beg of you," Nicholas whispered.

Maggie cried out, heartbroken, and Linny swore at the witch in three different languages. Ally stepped away from Maeve and stared dumbly at Aiden. She shook her head and mouthed, "No."

That image of her remained in his head, even as the sickening spinning began. Around and around, into darkness, the years passing them by. Closer and closer he came to his death, while happiness retreated behind him.

Chapter Thirty-Two

1808 Blackfriars Abbey,
Lincolnshire, England

DISORIENTATED, AIDEN, LORNE, and Nicholas stumbled up from the crypt, and the smell of burning grew stronger. Above them, the smoke thickened as they reached the house. Blackfriars Abbey must be ablaze.

"I wish I was home!" Nicholas shouted, and they knew he didn't mean at the Hellfire Club. Home was somewhere else now, and their hearts were there too.

"The Abbey is on fire." Lorne sounded winded. "They've set it on fire!"

The rational part of Aiden couldn't really blame the villagers. They were probably fed up after their wayward daughters had been lured from home to the crypt, followed by the Destroyer rampaging through the countryside and leaving a trail of dead bodies.

The front doors were wide open and they paused to stare out.

"They're building a bonfire of your belongings," Aiden said.

It turned out the fire was in the Abbey grounds, and the villagers had carried the furniture and various other flammable items out to throw upon it. As a Turkish rug was tossed onto the flames, voices were raised in cheers and jeers.

"Hoi!" The shout behind them made them turn. Two men were coming down the stairs from the gallery, carrying Lorne's portrait.

Lorne's icy blue eyes turned to fury.

"Put that down!" he ordered.

Such was his demeanour the men went to do his bidding, before they remembered why they were here. Then they tossed the portrait aside and called for their fellows. "They're here! The bloody toffs are here!"

The men around the bonfire were startled into action. Lorne, Nicholas and Aiden exchanged a brief look.

"Run!" Lorne shouted.

They set off across the green lawns of the Abbey with the pack baying after them. "Might I suggest that shouting at the people who wish to see us dead was a bad idea?" Nicholas puffed.

"Not now, Nicholas!"

It occurred to Aiden that as they were changed men, they should stop and offer their apologies, promise to make amends, but these fellows were unlikely to listen to reason. Aiden and his friends would be strung up from one of the old trees in the park. An eye for an eye was the only law these angry villagers understood.

I don't want to die, he thought. I want to get back to Ally.

Was that even a possibility? Probably not, but while there was life there was surely hope?

A stone hit him in the back and he yelped. They were almost at the line of trees that marked the beginning of the woods. At least they would have some shelter there. Something ran past them like the wind, and Aiden's heart both leapt and sank when he saw it was Loki. The hound seemed to think this was just another game.

They were in the trees now, but the mob hadn't given up and were still on their tail. Zig-zagging through the tree trunks, they tried to keep their footing, although Nicholas was limping badly and lagging behind.

Ahead was a woodsman's hut. Not the one Maggie had stayed in when she came to dig up the Abbey cemetery and found the Destroyer. This was a smaller one, long since gone by the time Maggie arrived. When they reached it, Lorne paused for a moment and then stopped to let Nicholas catch up.

They had a few brief minutes before the rabble would reach them. The Marquis looked at both his friends. "We deserve this," he said. "Part of the price of becoming better men is recognising that truth."

Although Nicholas seemed about to protest, he bit the words back and nodded curtly. "Yes," he said, "we do."

Aiden wanted to argue the point, but now he wondered what the point was. Lorne was right. They had brought this on themselves. With a nod of his own, he followed the other two inside.

The hut was hardly luxurious, built of split logs and windowless, with an earthen floor. At least the door had a solid bar. They used it because, as Nicholas had said, "He wasn't about to be dragged out and strung up by those damned yokels." They were resigned to their fate, but they wanted it to be reasonably dignified, if being burnt to death in a hut could be called such. Better than dancing from a rope at any rate.

Nicholas and Aiden stood panting in the semi-dark, and Lorne searched around in a cupboard in the corner and brought out an earthenware jug.

"Kettering, the woodsman, likes a drop," he explained, a half smile on his otherwise serious face. "God knows what it is. He brews it himself. It might make things a little easier for us if we take a good swallow each."

When it came Aiden's turn, he understood why the other two were coughing and gasping so hard. The liquid burned all the way down and landed like a gunpowder explosion in his stomach. His head was nicely foggy after they had passed the jug around twice more. Outside, they could hear the shouts of villagers and the door was barely holding up against the pounding fists and kicking boots. Then they smelt the smoke.

"Burn 'em out like the rats they are!" someone said, and the chant was quickly taken up.

It couldn't be long now, Aiden decided. It would be all over soon. Just as the history books he'd read said: There can be no doubt that the three members of the Hellfire Club were burned to death by the mob until their remains were mere ashes.

"Here." Lorne offered the jug again. "I'm only sorry I won't be there to see my son born. To hold him. To kiss Maggie and thank her for helping me become someone worthy of love." His icy blue eyes swam with tears, but he turned away before they could fall.

"I was going to have that operation on my leg that Linny wanted," Nicholas mused. "It would have been nice not to be in constant pain."

"I don't know what I was planning." Aiden reached down to ruffle Loki's fur, feeling bittersweet about his companion's presence here. "I'd probably have stayed on Moyle if that's what Ally wanted. Hold the skeins of wool for her while she knitted." He grinned. "Grow old together."

Nicholas muttered something about 'bloody awful weather' referring to the climate on the island. Lorne held out his hand.

"You've been good friends to me. The best. Brothers. I'm glad we are leaving this world together. I only hope the Sorceress isn't waiting for us on the other side."

They clasped their hands together.

"Let our sleep be undisturbed this time," Nicholas said. "I'd rather not be reminded of what I've lost."

"Perhaps Ally can scry me in her mirror?" Aiden said. "I wouldn't mind haunting her now and again."

The smoke was getting thicker and now it was difficult to breathe. Loki howled. Aiden's eyes were stinging. At least, he thought, he couldn't smell brimstone. Stewart could have Hell all to himself. The lack of oxygen and the strong spirits were dragging him down into unconsciousness. Lorne and Nicholas had slumped together, and Loki was licking Aiden's face in a final goodbye.

He wasn't sure whether it was his imagination, or wishful thinking, but as his mind faded into darkness, he thought he heard a familiar voice and saw a flicker of blue light.

"You've done well, my boys. I give you long and happy lives…"

Present Day Glasgow, Scotland

"Maggie, you're breaking my hand!" Linny wriggled her fingers, eyeing her sister with concern. Machines beeped and hummed in the birthing suite. They had come into the hospital as soon as Maggie's waters had broken, but the birth was taking longer than expected. The Young Marquis seemed in no hurry to come out into the world which, considering what had happened to his father, was understandable.

No help to Maggie though, or to Linny, thought Ally, who was slumped on a chair by the wall. She had travelled down from Moyle the day before for a visit and now found herself here at the birth. She wasn't even sure if she should be here, but the sisters had dragged her into the taxi with them.

None of them were feeling in a celebratory mood, but life had to go on, even when some days you wish it wouldn't.

After the bloodbath of Stewart's monsters at the ceilidh, the Sorceress had appeared and, without listening to arguments or even allowing good-byes, had sent the three gentlemen back to their own time.

The women had been devastated. Linny had cursed and threatened the Sorceress until she collapsed sobbing on the ground. After cry-ing non-stop for days, Maggie had turned very quiet, and hadn't smiled since. And Ally… Ally had returned to her cottage and wondered if she would ever feel whole again. Even Loki had van-ished.

She went for walks along the beach, staring out to sea. Sometimes she felt all alone in the world. Even the blue man had gone, returned to his people. It felt as if the Sorceress had been kinder to him than Aiden.

She didn't even feel like she belonged here in the hospital. She had only known Aiden and his friends for days. Maggie and Linny had far more right to be mourning their partners. She felt as if she was here under false pretences.

"They do wriggle their way into your heart," Linny had said, before Maggie's waters broke. They had been sitting gloomily around a table in Linny's little house. She and Maggie had been liv-ing there since they returned from Moyle. "Then, before you know it, boom! You find yourself des-perately in love with someone you swore to keep at arm's length."

"I think I fell in love the moment Lorne leapt

out of that grave and tackled the Destroyer," Maggie said. "He told me to run, but I wouldn't. I wanted to stay and save him."

"Of course you wouldn't run," Linny retorted. "You never did anything he told you to. I fell in love with Nicholas when I saw him playing the ghost here in Glasgow, although I think I was halfway there already."

"And what about you?" Maggie asked Ally. "When did you fall in love with Aiden?"

Ally stared at her. "I... I only knew him a few days."

Linny scoffed. "That doesn't mean anything. We're talking exceptional circumstances and exceptional men. Come on, when?"

Ally tried to think of the moment she lost her heart, but there were so many moments, small increments that added up to the whole. In the end she said, "When he first kissed me in the crypt, when we went back to the Hellfire Club."

The women nodded and sighed. One thing they all agreed on, life seemed very dull without the Hellfire Club boys.

The three of them had looked up the Hellfire Club on the internet, and read the descriptions of the wicked Marquis and his friends. There had been a statement from a local magistrate about their fate. It was presumed a fire had killed them, and ashes were all that remained of their bodies. It made depressing reading. Even the hot chocolate with marshmallows Linny had made and insisted they drink hadn't helped lift their spirits.

Now at the hospital, the nurse checked Maggie's vital signs, one eye on the baby's heartbeat, as another contraction started and she encouraged Maggie to push, and then as it waned, to pant. Maggie did as she was told but Linny could tell her heart wasn't in it. Her heart hadn't been in anything since Lorne went back.

Ally sat huddled in the corner, out of the way. She did love Aiden, she admitted it to herself. She loved him with all her heart. It didn't matter that it had only been a few days, she had lost her heart to a man who was never coming back. A tear ran down her cheek.

There was suddenly a commotion outside the door of the birthing suite.

They could hear one of the nurses refusing to let someone in, and then a voice was raised. A posh and imperious voice they knew very well. Maggie's eyes popped open. She half sat up, despite the nurse's protests. Her gaze went to the door.

"Lorne?" she gasped. Then, "Lorne!"

The door was flung open and there stood Lorne, flanked by Nicholas and Aiden. Loki rushed through and bounded around the bed. For a moment it was complete chaos, and then Lorne was there and Maggie was in his arms, and Linny flung herself at Nicholas. Aiden was staring into space and he looked melancholy… In her corner Ally stood up slowly, using the chair back as support.

"Aiden?" she whispered.

When he turned and saw her, his face lit up with joy. Aiden ran to her and picked her up, swinging her around and almost knocking over a piece of hospital equipment.

"We're back!" he said, his dark eyes wild with excitement.

Laughter bubbled up inside her. "I can see! What took you so long?"

Aiden looked confused. "But... it was only a few hours. What do you mean?"

Linny seemed to be having the same conversation with Nicholas. "It was months, Mister Earl!" she said loudly. "Four bloody months!"

The three men turned to each other in bewilderment. Lorne sighed. "We only just arrived outside the door. The Sorceress has been playing with time again," he said. Aiden wondered why, but when it came to the Sorceress, her own amusement was often reason enough.

Maggie groaned as another contraction built. Lorne's eyes widened. "My love?"

"The baby... your son is coming!" she said, looking flushed and flustered.

Two nurses had battled their way to the bed, trying to restore some sort of order. "Gentlemen, you have to leave!"

"He's the father," Maggie cut in. The glare she gave would have made even Stewart cower. The nurses made the best of the situation.

Lorne was enlisted into action to hold on to Maggie's hand, while an embarrassed Loki had been banished, along with the other four.

Nicholas took two steps down the corridor before he wrapped Linny in his arms. Aiden and Ally left them to it, and took Loki outside. "We were burning, or at least we thought we were," he explained. "We must have lost consciousness, because next thing we were here, outside the hospital room. Lorne guessed what it was all about. I hoped you would be here too, but I couldn't be sure."

Ally clung to his hand. "The police have been all over Moyle, trying to find out what happened in the ballroom that night. They think there was an attempt at mass murder, and hallucinogenic gas was used to send everyone trapped in the room crazy, imagining monsters and killing each other in the chaos. I think the survivors were happy to go along with it. My mother couldn't wait to get away. Apart from the ballroom the hotel wasn't damaged, and there's already talk about repurposing it. Turning it into a museum or a library, for the community. Now that Stewart... Frazer or whatever he called himself is dead, and he didn't leave a will... I suppose he thought he would live forever. But now the island will be returned to the people."

Aiden was listening in silence. "We've missed a lot," he said at last. "I can't believe it's been months."

"It felt like years," Ally admitted. Her eyes flooded with tears. "We missed you so much. I missed you."

He wrapped his arms around her. "It's all right," he murmured, holding her tight. "I'm here now. Back for good."

"No more tasks from our witchy friend?" she managed, wiping at her damp eyes and stepping away from him.

"No." He was watching her with a gentle smile. "We're done."

"What will you do with your lives now?"

He grinned but there was a vulnerable edge to it. "I thought I might go home with you. If you'll have me."

She didn't hesitate in her answer. "Yes."

She might have said more, but Nicholas was calling them back to the delivery room. When they reached the suite, Maggie and Lorne were squished together on the bed, the baby in Maggie's arms. She looked tired but so happy, and Lorne was flush with emotion. He lifted his head as they entered.

"I have a daughter," he said, choking on the words. "A little girl."

"We have a Marchioness," Linny announced, wiping her ears.

The others came to offer their congratulations, gathering around the new parents. Ally caught Aiden's eye and smiled. As he reached for her hand, she wondered whether this would be them one day. A child or two, a family, a life on distant Moyle. It would be a very quiet life, but she thought Aiden would be happy with that.

Only time, and the Sorceress, would tell.

About the Author

Sara Mackenzie is the author of
The Immortal Warriors series and other
Paranormal romances.
https://www.saramackenzie.com/

While you're there sign up to her Newsletter
for the latest news:
*www.facebook.com/saramackenzieparanormalro-
mance/app/152926008054123*

You can also visit her on her Facebook page:
*www.facebook.com/saramackenzieparanormalro-
mance*

Look for these titles by
Sara Mackenzie

NOW AVAILABLE:

Return of the Highlander
Secrets of the Highwayman
Passions of the Ghost
Heart of the Gunslinger

Hellfire Club: Lorne (1)
Hellfire Club: Darlington (2)
Hellfire Club: Sutcliffe (3)

Stepping Back
Castle on the Loch

COMING SOON:

With My Last Breath

www.ingramcontent.com/pod-product-compliance
Lightning Source LLC
Chambersburg PA
CBHW072356110726
47909CB00003B/720